# CROOKED CREEK

A WESTERN

ROBERT HANLON

ISBN: 9781521324981

# CHAPTER ONE

The stranger rode into town late in the afternoon. It had been a long ride from Silverton to this godforsaken one-horse cow pie of a place, Heaven Brook. From the looks of things, this place was rebuilding itself after having been burned down. Over half the buildings looked partially constructed, and the other half appeared to have been burned down recently. The only place in town that looked nearly complete was the hotel. But upon further inspection, the stranger saw that only the front half of the building was complete. The back half still needed a roof and windows.

He rode up and tied off his horse to a rail in front of a large tent with a sign over the doorway that read "Saloon." Sliding off his horse, he dusted himself off, but when he walked away, he still left a trail of dust behind him. Despite the dirt, there was no mistaking his deerskin pants and shirt. His boots, under a thick layer of powdered earth, were black with a shiny tin plate on the toes and heel. His brown hat was ordinary and just as dusty as the rest of him. As he walked up to the door, he looked up and down the muddy street and saw no one, not even a stray dog. "Nice" was the only word he mumbled to himself as he opened the saloon door and stepped inside.

The inside of the saloon wasn't much better than the outside. It was dirty and damp. The canvas of the tent flapped when the wind blew. The bar was off to the left, what there was of it. It was ten feet long and set up on top of two big barrels with a few boards tacked on the front to keep them steady. The countertop was made of some sort of solid rock that was polished smooth. Behind the makeshift bar was a mirror nailed to a big wood frame above a half-dozen shelves filled with dusty glasses, plates and mugs. The top shelf held a dozen bottles of the same rotgut whiskey lined up with their labels all facing forward. At the far end of the bar, on a makeshift table made from a couple of planks on top of a couple of smaller barrels, was what appeared to be a barrel of beer laying on its side. Next to it were several dozen glasses just as dusty as the trail.

The stranger walked up to the bar and stood there for a minute waiting to be served, using the mirror to look around the place. There wasn't much to see. There was an old man sleeping on a couple of chairs over by the potbelly stove. To complete the saloon's attractions were four men dressed in dirty, dusty clothes. They were playing poker at a table against the far wall of the place.

"Is the sleeping man the bartender?" the stranger asked the four men. The men ignored him, and the sleeping man continued to sleep. The stranger waited another minute or two before giving up, and just when he was about to go get his own drink, an older man with a potbelly of his own and a big gray mustache stepped into the tent through a side entrance.

"Howdy, stranger. New in town?" the old man greeted.

"Nope, been here my whole life," the stranger replied with a smirk.

At first, the man was taken aback by the stranger's sarcastic comment, but he warmed up and grinned at the stranger. "I see you're one of those men who likes to make funny comments. That was a good one. But… I'd be careful who you share your sense of humor with around here. Too many people hereabouts take themselves far too seriously," the old man warned. "Now, what can I get you?"

"Without laughter in your life, it ain't hardly worth living," the stranger replied. "A beer would be good."

"A beer it is. So, what brings you to Heaven Brook?" the old man asked as he drew a beer from the keg.

"I'm here for work. Know of any?" the stranger asked. He noticed the four men playing cards all looked up at him.

"Work? Here? No, sir, I'm afraid you may have been misled," the old man said loudly and then stood there, looking uncomfortable.

"Are you telling me no one's going to finish building those buildings?" the stranger asked, gesturing outside. The four men slid back their chairs quietly, although what they were doing was easy enough for the stranger to see in the mirror.

"Well, there's been some talk of relocating the town. The water ain't so good," the old man said as he stepped several steps away and started wiping dust off some of the glasses.

"I see. I guess I was misinformed. Is there any place in town where a man might get a shave, a bath and a good meal?" the stranger asked.

"The only place in town with anything close to that is the hotel across the street. They have a barber, a bathhouse and a cook. Whether the cook's any good... well, I'll leave that up to you to decide."

"What about a place to board my horse for the night?" the stranger asked. The four men playing cards stood up and stared at him. They were hard-looking men with dirty clothes, dirty hands, dirty hair and every one of them needing shaves and haircuts. Their faces were covered with rough beards, busted up noses and bad teeth, all wrapped in scowls.

"Sure thing. There's a livery stable at the end of the street." The old man pointed off to his left. The stranger dropped two bits on the counter for the beer and started for the door.

One of the four men at the table with a salt and pepper beard called out to him. "What line of work have you done before?" he asked as the four men spread themselves out in a line blocking the door.

The stranger stopped and slowly turned around to face them. "I've been doing some collecting as of late," he replied without showing any expression.

"Collecting? Collecting what?" the salt and pepper bearded man asked. It was now the stranger noticed a large jagged scar running down the side of his face. Yep, that was the distinguishing feature he was looking for.

"Oh, mostly dead stuff," the stranger said and then smiled at the man.

"Dead stuff? What are you talkin' about?" another man with an ugly scar asked, obviously not comprehending what the stranger was saying.

"Well, you see, I collect a bunch of papers, and these papers tell me what I'm to collect and where it is."

"What? Where do you get these papers from?" the man next asked.

"I get them at the sheriff's office."

"The sheriff's office?" the man questioned, then looked at his friends briefly before turning back to the stranger. "Like a bounty hunter?"

"Exactly like a bounty hunter," the stranger replied, though he didn't make any apparent move to reach for his gun. "Do you know anyone around here with a bounty on their head?" he asked.

All four men exchanged glances and then they started shaking their heads and mumbling, "No… we don't know anyone like that…" Suddenly, all four men reached for their guns and the stranger did the same. Before any of them could draw their guns, the stranger drew and fired his six-shooter four times. Within seconds, all four men fell to the floor, dead. In the end, only one of the four had managed to fire his gun. The bullet had gone into the floor by the stranger's feet.

The stranger walked over to the men and stood over them, looking at their faces. He pulled a handful of papers from his pocket and began flipping through them. After a few moments, he began pulling pieces of paper out of the handful, laying a single sheet on each man's chest. As he did so, he rifled through their clothes and collected any money he found. He also removed their gun belts.

When he had finished putting the papers on the men and collecting everything of value from them, he placed the gun belts on the bar and asked the bartender to hold them for him. "You got an undertaker in this town?" he asked.

"Why, yes, sir. We do," the bartender replied nervously.

"Good. Could you ask him to wrap up these bodies in their bedrolls, making sure they're tied up nice and neat. I'll be taking the bodies with me when I leave tomorrow," the stranger instructed him, then flipped the man a twenty dollar gold piece. "Keep the change," he said as he walked out the door.

"Hey, mister, I didn't get your name," the bartender called after him.

"That's right. You didn't," the stranger replied as he untied his horse and started walking towards the livery stables.

## *CHAPTER TWO*

The stranger dropped off his horse at the livery and filled out the forms needed to claim the horses of the four men who had just died in the saloon. Afterwards, he made arrangements for a hot bath, a shave, a hot meal, and a room for the night.

It was while he was getting his shave that a white- haired man, who was of average height but fifty pounds overweight, came along and introduced himself.

"Evening, sir. I don't mean to interrupt, but it's my job as sheriff to address what happened in the saloon an hour ago," the heavy-set, white-haired man said while gripping the handle of his gun.

"Oh, hello. And you are?" the stranger asked.

"I'm the sheriff of Heaven Brook, Kevin Nape, and I'm going to have to ask you for your gun. We don't abide bounty hunters, or anyone else for that matter, coming into our town and shooting up the place. In fact, you're in violation of our ordinance against carrying guns in town. That's a five dollar fine," the sheriff stuttered slightly as he spoke. He was holding the handle of his gun so tightly, his knuckles were white.

"Well, Sheriff Nape, were the men I shot in violation of your ordinance too?" the stranger asked.

"Well, no. They live here and have a license to carry," the sheriff replied.

"And what does a license cost, Sheriff?" the stranger asked as the barber continued to shave him.

"It's only a dollar, but if it's retroactive, such as yours would be, then it's... ahh... with the infraction and all... it's... ahh... well, you see, it's the ordinance that requires it and it would be... ahh—"

"Sheriff, I think it's time for you to leave. Don't come back unless you want to explain yourself to the Honorable Milton Westbrook, the Chief Justice of the Territorial Court. He's been charged by the territorial governor with cleaning up the backlog of wanted men in the territory. I work directly for the judge, and the piece of paper in my pocket says I'm not obliged to enforce or operate under any local law or ordinance. I also have the power to arrest, detain or execute criminal individuals as I see fit, including any local law enforcement or locally elected or appointed officials, who attempt in any way to interfere in my official duties. That would include you, sir, running your mouth off to anyone about my position with the territorial court. Now, Sheriff, have I made myself clear?" the stranger stated authoritatively.

Sheriff Nape, a man afraid of his own shadow, slowly backed out of the room and then hurriedly walked down the hallway to the front door. Once he had stepped outside, he was confronted by two men blocking his path. They were big enough to warrant being designated as small mountains and looked as mean as a couple of rattlesnakes.

"Well?" one of the men, wearing a black hat, asked the sheriff.

"He's a bounty hunter, and I doubt I can handle him. He looks real mean. I'd stay away from him if I were you," the sheriff cautioned as he quickly stepped around them and walked off down the street.

The two men watched the sheriff walk away. Then they went into the hotel and met up with the stranger walking into the dining hall. They walked over to where they would be purposely blocking the stranger from reaching his table. The stranger immediately knew they were someone's hired muscle and decided he wasn't going to let them stop him from enjoying his dinner. Finding his table blocked by the human boulders, the stranger stopped between them and started a conversation.

"And who might you be? The deceased's next of kin?"

"What? No! Our boss wants to meet with you right now," the man in the black hat replied.

"Gee, that's too bad. Go back to your boss and tell him I'm busy eating my dinner. He's welcome to join me, but he's to leave you two at home. Goons make me nervous, and I tend to shoot people if I get too nervous," the stranger said as he tried to walk around the man, but the man wouldn't move. He just stood there glaring at him.

"What's the matter? Cat got your tongue?" the stranger asked.

"Mr. Winters doesn't like to be kept waiting. Your dinner will have to wait," the man said and put his hand on his gun for emphasis.

The stranger turned to the other man and cocked his head. "So, what do you weigh, three hundred pounds?"

"What? How should I know?" the man responded as he patted himself, as if that might tell him how much he weighed.

"I was just wondering," the stranger said as he turned back to the man in the black hat. "So, you men eat a lot of beef?"

"What? Why are you asking such strange questions?" the man replied as he glared at the stranger.

"Oh, I'm just killing time while I decide which one of you to put down first," he said and then stomped on the big man's right foot as hard as he could. He spun around and lashed out, kicking the other man in the shin, then stomping on his foot as well. With both men now hopping, each on one foot, the stranger promptly kicked both men in the groin. The two big men collapsed on the floor, grabbing their groins. The stranger reached down and pulled a gun from each of their holsters. He then stepped over the man in the black hat as he made his way to his table. As he sat down, he waved to the server to bring out his meal.

The stranger sat on the far side of the table so he could see when the two men got up. It wouldn't do to have one of those man mountains get behind him where they could sneak up and twist off his head. The server had just put steak and mashed potatoes down in front of him when the two men got up. They stood glaring at the stranger who continued eating. With every chew, their frustration grew until it got the better of them. The one who had been wearing the black hat roared, grabbed the table in front of him, lifted it up and tossed it aside. The stranger's eyes went wide as he scooped a mouthful of buttery mashed potatoes into his mouth, but the display of anger hardly slowed his feeding frenzy.

As the table flew, he casually picked up the gun he'd left laying on the table in front of him and pointed it at the big man. He took only two steps before he realized the stranger had a gun pointed at him. He then looked at his partner and they both got smirks on their faces. They charged, and the stranger promptly shot each man in his right thigh, set the gun down, grabbed a piece of bread and continued eating his dinner.

Each man lay on the floor, howling in pain and anger for a moment or two before jumping up on his one good leg.

Together they began hopping towards the stranger again. This time when the stranger pointed the gun at them he called out, "One more step and I'll be turning a couple of bulls into heifers." Both men stopped in their tracks.

"Since you gentlemen have been so rude, you can tell your boss if he wants to meet me, he should come by the saloon, and we'll have a drink together." As an afterthought, the stranger added, "You two definitely stay home."

When the two men didn't move, the stranger waved the gun and told them to "get." The man who wore the black hat turned to go and said, "This ain't over."

"Oh, goodie, more entertainment to come," the stranger replied mockingly.

The stranger finished his dinner in peace. When he got up to leave, he handed the server ten dollars for the meal and ten dollars for the damages. He then strolled out of the hotel and walked down the street with a six-gun in each hand.

## *CHAPTER THREE*

The stranger had been nursing his beer and playing solitaire in the empty saloon for almost an hour when a man stepped through the front door. He was clean shaven, had a fresh haircut, and was dressed in clean clothes. He was followed by a group of four men. Each one was dirty, unshaven, in need of a haircut and wore a permanent sneer on his face.

The group of men spread out in a line across the room while the man walked over to where the stranger was sitting and stared at him. He waited for the stranger to acknowledge him, but the stranger continued playing solitaire, minding his own business.

Finally, the man spoke. "You're the stranger in town, aren't you?"

"I guess nothing gets past you, considering I'm the only man in the place," the stranger replied curtly.

"I'm—" the man began.

"No, wait, don't tell me. Let me see if my powers of observation are as good as yours. "Hmmm... let's see... You're dressed in clean clothes, your hands aren't covered in calluses, you're clean-shaven, and you've recently had a haircut. You project power when you come into a room with four hired guns behind you. So, that must mean you're Mr. Winters." The stranger smirked and went back to playing cards.

"I expect people to look at me when I speak to them," said Winters, obviously thinking the stranger could be intimidated by his tone.

"Well, then, I guess we won't be having a conversation," the stranger replied. He reached out with his right hand and touched one of the two six-guns laying on the table.

"What?" Winters blurted out loudly. The four men all took a step forward while grabbing for their guns. In the flash of an eye, the stranger picked up the six-gun and pointed it at Winters. Winters instantly got the message and quickly waved his hand for the four goons to step back.

"I have a business proposition for you," Winters informed him as his men backed away.

"What kind? I sort of have a job," the stranger replied and continued playing solitaire.

"That's not what I hear. I heard you were looking for work," Winters told him.

"Well, that was before I stumbled upon a tidy bankroll."

"Yes, because of you, I'm down four men. They were good at what they did, and now I'll have to find four more at considerable expense," Winters stated.

"Really? I hope you kept your receipt. They were defective merchandise, if I ever saw it," the stranger replied.

"You also beat up and shot two of my personal bodyguards. The doctor's bill is going to be at least a hundred dollars," Winters said angrily.

"They're awfully big fellows. Maybe you could sell them based on a price per pound. I'd bet they'd bring at least two bits a pound. Of course, any good buyer will want a discount due to them being lame and all," the stranger retorted sarcastically.

Winters was struggling not to step aside and have his four bodyguards start blasting away at this smart- mouthed man, but he hung in there, and after taking a deep breath, continued, "May I at least know your name, sir?" he asked in a calm voice.

"Sure. I was wondering if anyone in this town would bother to ask. I'm Jake Timber. People call me Timber."

"May I sit down, Timber?"

"Please, be my guest. Care for a beer? How about a whiskey?" Timber offered.

"A whiskey would be fine," Winters replied.

Timber called out to the bartender and told him to bring over a bottle of his best whiskey, something unopened, and two glasses, dusted. The bartender hopped out of his chair behind the bar and hurried over.

When he had set the bottle and glasses down on the table, Timber told him, "Good man. Be sure to give the peanut gallery a drink on me as well." He tossed him a ten dollar silver piece. The bartender hurried off to do as he was told.

"I see you're a generous man," Winters remarked as the old man retreated.

"I once had real money, and I know what it's like to work for nearly nothing, so I like to treat the people who serve me well," Timber replied, continuing his game of solitaire.

Winters poured himself a drink and downed it as he watched Timber play. After a minute or so had passed, he asked, "Why wouldn't you come with the men I sent earlier?"

"They caught me at dinner, and they weren't polite about it."

"They're not paid to be polite. I don't generally wait on anyone or anything," Winters shared.

"Then I can tell you right now, I can't work for you. I have a bit of trouble with authority."

"I can make it worth your while," Winters spoke confidently.

"Oh, how can you do that?" Timber asked as he reached for his gun again. He had noticed one of the four goons starting to move towards his far right side. Seeing Timber's move, Winters put up his hand and waved the man back to the bar. The man reluctantly moved back.

"Do you really think you could get the drop on these four men like you did the four this afternoon?" Winters asked as he poured a second drink.

"I'd bet I'd stand a fair chance, but I wouldn't go there right away. I'd shoot you first because you're so much easier to hit when you're sitting next to me," Timber informed him.

Winters set his drink down. He clearly wasn't amused. He called out to his men. "Stop moving around. You're interfering with my conversation. Stay at the bar and have another drink or two." The men turned back to the bar and poured another round.

Winters took a deep breath. "You see, Timber, I need a man who is willing to get a little dirty and won't worry about who gets hurt as long as he gets paid for his services. By the way, I pay very well."

"The job I've got pays very well. It's incredible how much it pays based on the few hours I work on a steady basis. It also affords me a good deal of leisure time. I can go hunting or fishing whenever I choose," Timber replied.

"The four men you shot today, were they all wanted men?" Winters asked.

"They worked for you, and you don't know?" Timber found it hard to believe that that was the case.

"In my business, it's usually best to leave those penetrating questions unasked. Who among us has a pristine past?" Winters stated in his defense.

"And what business are you in anyway?" Timber asked pointedly.

"I hear tell you told the bartender that you were in collecting, and I guess if pressed, I'd have to say I'm in acquisitions. I like to acquire things without paying for them," Winters responded as he picked up his drink and downed it.

"Offhand, it appears we're on opposite sides, Winters. But I'm still listening," Timber said as he took a swig of his warm beer.

"The way I figure it, we're both in it to make money, and we'll both stop at nothing to get it. So, we're not that different. Right and wrong are merely one's own perspective, and it frequently changes with the opportunities that present themselves." Winters went on, "Take those four men again. What did you get for a bounty on them? Three or four hundred dollars per head? I can pay you twice that each month, if you'll help me make my acquisitions."

Timber stopped playing cards and reached into his pocket. He pulled out his wad of wanted posters and flipped through them until he found the four men from the afternoon and spread them on the table.

"As you can see, they're worth considerably more than three or four hundred dollars. They had bounties of five hundred dollars each on their heads. They were bank robbers, thieves, murderers and rapists," Timber told him, ticking off their crimes.

"That's far more than I would have guessed," Winters commented. "I can pay a thousand a month for a year at least, if you'll join me right now."

"It's tempting, but I have these bodies to haul in that are worth two thousand dollars right now. After I get that done, I think I'll take you up on the offer," Timber told him.

"I can't wait until you get back here. I need the help now!" Winters practically shouted. His men turned towards the table again and stared at the two of them.

"I'm sorry, but I can't walk away from two thousand dollars," Timber replied.

Winters wiped his upper lip with the back of his hand. He stared intently at Timber who ignored him and continued playing cards.

Finally, with his frustration growing, Winters blurted out, "Allow me the courtesy of seeing you in the morning before you leave, so I might make you another offer."

"I'm looking to be on the trail by nine, so you'll need to send word or come to the hotel yourself to discuss it well before then," Timber told him.

Winters pushed back his chair, stood up, and walked away. His entourage turned and followed him out.

## *CHAPTER FOUR*

"You're not seriously considering going to work for him, are you?" the bartender asked as he picked up the partially drunk bottle of whiskey and the dirty glass.

"No, not really, but I couldn't be so cruel as to disappoint the man twice in one day," Timber replied with a smirk on his face. "Say," Timber changed the subject, "can you quickly run over to the undertaker and give him this?" He handed the old man a twenty dollar gold piece. "Tell him I'd like to know where he buries those four bodies. Also, ask him to somehow mark each grave so the bodies can be easily recovered in a few days."

"You think Winters will try to steal them? Why?" the old man asked.

"Absolutely. He hates to be told no, and if I don't have any bodies to deliver for the big bounty, he figures I'll be desperate for work, and I'll be a lot cheaper hire. Now, get to the undertaker before Winters' men do," Timber ordered.

In the meantime, Winters was walking back to his place. He was almost there before he decided to do just as Timber suspected he would.

"Bond," Mr. Winters barked and his hired hand, Jack Bond, quickly stepped up to attention.

"Yes, sir," Bond responded as though he was still in the military.

"Bond, get over to the undertaker's and tell him to get rid of those four bodies he's holding for Timber. Tell him I want them buried well away from town where no one will find them. You got that?"

"Yes, sir. Take the four bodies and bury them away from town where no one will find them," Bond repeated.

"Good. Now get!" Winters ordered, and Bond took off at a trot.

Meanwhile, the old bartender had given the undertaker the twenty dollars and explained what Timber wanted him to do. Five minutes later, Bond arrived and gave him Winters' instructions. He didn't offer the undertaker any money but threatened to harm him if he didn't do as he was told.

The choice was an easy one to make. The undertaker would make it look as though he had buried four bodies somewhere out of town but, in reality, the graves would be marked so that Timber would be able to find them in a few days. The undertaker had but one motto by which he ran his business—you've got to pay to play. Winters never paid, so he wasn't about to let him play.

****

Timber spent another long, restless night alternating between shallow napping and nightmares. It had been his lot in life for the past few years. The nightmares were the same every night. A woman was screaming in fear. He was running through a dark alley trying to find her. Men kept stepping out from the shadows, blocking his path and trying to kill him. They came running at him from all directions, diving at him from every shadow and blocking his path at every turn. The harder he fought, the more men appeared, and the woman's screams grew louder and louder until he awoke and sat bolt upright in bed, clawing at his side for his gun.

From the first night it happened, and each and every night since, he struggled to sleep more than an hour or two at a time. Many nights he'd pass on sleeping completely. Instead, he'd take his horse and go for a long ride, returning just as the sun was rising. When he had been in prison, he had spent the nights sitting in the dark, reliving the hellish nightmare his life had become while weeping silently in his cell.

His life regained its purpose when a man, calling himself a judge, offered him a pardon, provided he would channel his special skills to do good for society as a whole and set aside his personal vendetta. It had been the most difficult decision he'd ever had to make. In the end, he figured it would be better to fight the good fight in the daylight rather than fight an unreachable, unbeatable foe in the dark each night.

Upon his release, the judge handed him a piece of paper and swore him in as a special agent of the court. He then turned him loose to wander about the territory eliminating those among society who were predators and criminals. He wasn't charged with bringing them to court for trial but rather to disperse justice from the barrel of a gun. If you were wanted by the law, or should have been, he was authorized to administer justice with all the lethality he could muster. The ultimate goal was to clean up the territory so it might look its best when applying for statehood.

****

First thing in the morning, Timber made a show of going to the undertaker's and screaming at him for his incompetence before slipping him another twenty dollars. He stomped back to the hotel, continuing to bemoan the man's incompetence. Losing four bodies in one night had to be some sort of an historical record, even for a one-horse town like Heaven Brook.

Timber had just finished a huge breakfast of mouthwatering biscuits and gravy when Winters and his four goons walked in. No one said hello or openly looked at them as they walked through the dining room to where Timber was sitting in the corner with his back to the wall. He didn't have a gun laying on the table this morning, but he did have one laying in his lap under a napkin.

As Winters arrived at the table, Timber greeted him. "Well, imagine my surprise to see the one and only Mr.

Winters this morning. Good morning, sir." Timber almost made it sound sincere.

"Cut the crap, Timber. I hear your situation has changed," Winters curtly responded.

"Oh, how's that?"

"We both know that someone broke into the undertaker's last night and stole those four bodies you were interested in. It's too bad you lost all that money. Has anyone stolen your bounties before?" Winters asked, clearly gloating over the perceived situation.

"No, I can't say anyone has," Timber replied as he took the last gulp of his coffee.

"So, are you going to continue searching for more outlaws and hope you can get them turned in before something happens to their bodies, or should we consider bringing you into the fold of the Winters family?" Winters' tone had certainly changed since last night when he wanted him at almost any cost.

"I'll work for you, provided it's on a part-time basis. Plus, you'll need to pay me fifty dollars a day when I do work, unless it's a big job. Then I want a fair cut of the loot," Timber told him.

"Those are some pretty bold demands," Winters responded.

"And I'm worth every last penny and then some. Of course, if it's too steep a price for you, I'll do just fine collecting my bounties."

"Timber, you're going to insult me one too many times, and I'll be forced to have you killed," Winters snarled.

"As they say in New York, you can try, but I doubt you'll have any luck," Timber snarled in return.

"You don't get it, do you?" Winters barked at Timber. "I'm a very rich and powerful man in these parts, and I don't suffer fools well."

"That's another thing we have in common. It's almost as if we were a working partnership waiting to happen, except I doubt either one of us works well with people in authority. We both figure if someone is going to be in charge, it ought to be us." Timber smirked.

"I'll give you a little bit of advice, Timber. I strongly suggest that you leave our town as soon as possible."

"As much as leaving this garden spot would pleasure me, I have obligations that I simply can't walk away from. Though I will promise you, I'll get right to it and only stay as long as necessary." Timber finished his coffee and set the cup down on the table. He stood up, tucking the second gun in his gun belt and started to walk away, but one of Winters' men blocked his path.

"Oh, by the way," Timber acted as though he had forgotten something, and the man blocking him didn't warrant any direct attention yet, "did you know that grave robbing is a criminal offense even if the bodies aren't actually buried yet? Whoever took the bodies or caused them to be stolen has committed a felony that's punishable by up to five years in jail per body. You might just want to inform your sheriff of that. I doubt he's up on the latest laws of the territory, and unless you want to lose a few more men, I'd have the boulder here roll out of the way." Timber stared at Winters who, after a momentary hesitation, waved his hand, and the man stepped aside. "You all have a good day," Timber said, then turned and walked out.

He went to the front desk to arrange to stay another night while Winters and his men stormed out of the dining room and straight out the front door of the hotel. The clerk, who was also the owner of the hotel, watched Winters leave. He waited until the door had completely closed behind him before commenting.

"Mr. Winters don't look too happy. In fact, both times he met with you, he came away angrier than a snake with its tail nailed to a board," he observed.

"Some folk just can't be happy unless they control other people," Timber replied.

"Well, I'd watch your back if I were you. Winters meant it when he said he could have you killed."

"That's just a bullying tactic to try and control me," Timber absently commented.

"He does want to control you. Right along with everything else in this town. If he can't control you on his own, he'll take drastic steps to be able to do so."

"If that's the case, I'm sure he didn't sleep at all last night. He probably sees me as the harbinger of his losing control of this town. He may be right, but then he only has himself to blame. We all must reap the seeds we sow," Timber said as he walked away.

Stepping out of the hotel door, Timber found himself looking at a small, wiry man wearing glasses and dressed in a business suit and top hat.

## CHAPTER FIVE

"What are you dressed up for?" Timber asked.

"Very funny," the man stated curtly. "I'm Harold J. Castleman, Attorney at Law, and I represent Mr. Rogers."

"How nice for Mr. Rogers. What's it to me?" Timber asked as he stepped past the little man and began walking towards the livery. Mr. Castleman fell in line behind Timber and followed him.

"Mr. Timber, my employer, Mr. Rogers, asked me to contact you and invite you to his ranch for a meeting this afternoon."

"A meeting? What's the meeting about?" Timber asked as he came to a stop and pulled the papers from his pocket. He quickly thumbed through the sheets and stopped when he came to a particular one. He looked up, watching a man go into a saloon on the opposite side of the street.

"He would like to discuss hiring you to do a job for the citizens of Heaven Brook," Castleman said.

"Really, for the citizens of Heaven Brook? You already have a sheriff and a mayor, so what might I do for Heaven Brook?" Timber asked.

"I'm not at liberty to explain the offer, only to invite you to come and discuss it."

"What time does this little hoedown get started? I have some work to do here in town, but afterwards I believe I have time to meet the town's other most prominent citizen."

"Do you know the way to Mr. Rogers' ranch?" Castleman asked.

"Not to worry. I'll bet anyone around here can point me in the right direction," Timber responded as he pulled his gun and quickly made sure it was loaded before stuffing it back in its holster. "If you don't mind, I have to go and collect a bounty now." Timber walked away from Castleman and stepped into the saloon.

Unlike the saloon he had visited last night, this one had several customers at the bar and three tables full of men playing poker. It was nine in the morning, and it was already busy. A quick survey of the patrons and their drinks revealed that not one person was drinking coffee. It was all beer and whiskey.

Timber walked up to the bar. "What can I get you?" the bartender asked. He was an older man with nearly white hair and a potbelly.

"I'll take a coffee," Timber responded, "in a clean cup."

The bartender grinned widely and asked, "No, really, what can I get you?"

Timber repeated himself. "No, really, a coffee, black and in a clean cup."

"A clean cup. What a hoot. My buddy Zeb said you were a character," the bartender said but didn't move.

"Who's your buddy?"

"He's the owner and bartender across the street at the other saloon. His name is Zeb and I'm Keb."

"I see, Zeb and Keb. You family?" Timber asked, noticing the resemblance between the two men and the closeness of their names.

"Naw, just friends," Keb said in reply.

"So, Keb, how is it that you have so much business at nine in the morning, when your friend didn't have a soul at ten last night?" Timber asked as he studied the crowd in the large mirror behind the bar.

"Zeb doesn't play the game. You see, the power brokers around here require you provide them with a share of the profits in exchange for them ordering their people to utilize your business. I pay both those thieves, so I always have plenty of business."

"So, how much do they take?" Timber asked.

"Too much. Now, what can I get you? Whiskey, beer?" Keb asked again, avoiding the question.

"I'll have a coffee, black and in a clean cup," Timber repeated.

"Okay, but I don't recommend coffee. It has to do with the water around here. To get a real jump on the day, I prefer whiskey myself—wipes the cobwebs right out of your head with just one swallow," Keb informed him as he walked to the far end of the bar where there was a small cook stove with a coffee pot on it. He poured a cup and walked back, setting it on the bar in front of Timber. "It's in a clean cup, too." Keb smirked. Timber took a sip of the hot liquid, which tasted like rusty roofing tar, and set the cup down before asking a few questions.

"So, do all the local employers allow their men to drink before work?"

"Oh, hell, no. Most of these men work nights for Mr. Rogers."

"What work does Mr. Rogers have for these men to do at night?" Timber asked, but before Keb could answer, one of the men sitting at the other end of the bar interrupted.

"It would be best, Keb, if you told your new friend to mind his own business," the man said without turning to look at them. He was heavy-chested with large muscular arms and looked like he was a tall man.

"Oh, my, yes. I'm terribly sorry, Mr. Tanner. I just got carried away. I'm not awake yet," Keb nervously apologized and walked away from Timber.

"You must be a powerful man to cause the owner of this place to shut right down and walk away," Timber commented. He figured the day was young, and he needed some exercise to work the kinks out.

"Like I said, it's none of your business," the man growled.

"I just don't see how it's none of my business when I'm being polite and friendly. I'm just looking for work, that's all," Timber replied in a calm voice, trying to sound friendly.

"Drink your coffee and leave, or I'll help you out," the man said, flexing his muscles in his arms to emphasize the point.

"I'd say from the look of those arms you must be a miner or something," Timber replied, then for good measure added, "Or do you muck stalls all night?"

The man slammed down his shot glass, and everyone in the place except Timber jumped up and scurried to the far corners of the saloon. "Was it something I said?" Timber asked as he smirked at the man. That was all it took.

The man reached for his gun and spun to face Timber. Instead of backing off, Timber jumped right at him. As they collided, Timber grabbed the whiskey bottle off the top of the bar and smashed it into the middle of the man's face. The man, to his credit, only grunted in pain and then flung Timber off him. Timber landed in the group of tables in front of the fireplace, knocking tables and chairs every which way. When he hit the floor, he instinctively rolled over and pulled his gun. Before he could fire, Mr. Castleman stepped between them.

"Hold it, Tanner!" Castleman shouted in a voice that belied his size. Tanner froze, eyeing Castleman with pure malice, but he didn't make any further moves. He stood there with his gun half out of his holster and murder clearly on his mind.

"Mr. Rogers has business with this man. You will cease and desist until such time as Mr. Rogers or myself release you to settle whatever score you think you have with this man but not until then. Am I understood?" Castleman asked.

"Yes, sir, Mr. Castleman. I wasn't aware of Mr. Rogers' interest."

"No, I'm sure you weren't. In the future, to avoid any painful misunderstandings, you might want to check with the foreman before you instigate trouble you can't win," Mr. Castleman stated, turning to Timber. "I hope your business wasn't to disturb the peace so early in the morning."

"On the contrary. That man has a dead or alive bounty on his head. I really don't care which way I collect it, but I am going to collect it," Timber replied in no uncertain terms.

"I see. I suppose you have papers that back this claim of him being a wanted man?" Castleman inquired. Tanner tried to walk away, but Castleman held out his hand. "Stay right there, Tanner."

Timber pulled the wad of papers from his pocket and flipped through them until he found the right one. He handed it to Castleman who looked it over and then handed it back before ordering Tanner to go to the jailhouse with Timber so the sheriff could place him in a cell. Timber was flabbergasted. Tanner gave Castleman a look that would have killed most men, but Castleman simply said, "Do it now, Tanner, or we'll leave you there to be hanged."

"Drop the gun belt," Timber said. Tanner dropped his gun belt as instructed, staring at Castleman with daggers in his eyes. "Now, empty all your pockets." Tanner looked at Castleman as if the little man could or would somehow change his mind, but it didn't happen.

When Tanner had finished emptying his pockets and had put everything on the bar next to his gun belt, Timber told Keb, "Keep an eye on that. I expect it to still be here when I come back in a few minutes.

Tanner snarled, "If that stuff isn't here when I come back, I'll be sure to take my time taking their value out of your hide."

Timber slapped the back of Tanner's head, causing him to stumble a bit, then looked over at Keb and mouthed, "He's not coming back."

Timber walked Tanner across the street to the sheriff's office with a gun aimed at his back. Castleman followed close behind.

Once there, Timber made sure the sheriff understood that Tanner was his prisoner and that he wasn't to receive any visitors other than his lawyer. The sheriff told Timber that since he was just holding Tanner for him, it would cost him five dollars a day to cover the cost of food and guards around the clock. Timber said he would get it from the bounty money, and was told he had until the end of the day to pay for the next five days in total. There would be no refund should Timber decide to leave earlier, or the sheriff would simply turn Tanner loose.

Timber gave the sheriff a nasty look and walked out without agreeing to anything. Upon returning to the saloon, Timber saw Keb had taken everything off the bar, probably tucking it underneath on a shelf.

Timber was in a good mood and decided to have some fun. He yelled, "Anyone else a wanted man?" The ten or so men still in the saloon all quickly hurried out the back door, causing Timber to observe, "Wow, a town full of law abiding citizens."

"It's all right here, Mr. Timber," Keb said as he reached under the bar and grabbed Tanner's belongings and set them on top of the bar. Timber stepped up and gave Keb an inquiring look.

"That's all of it except the twenty-two dollars he ran up on a tab. I left the other ten dollars he had with the gun belt as you ordered," Keb explained, but he didn't look Timber in the eye as he did so.

"That's not quite what I told you, Keb, but if he legitimately owes you twenty-two dollars, then that's all right. Did he honestly owe you twenty-two dollars?" Timber asked as he stared intently at Keb.

"Well, yes, he..." Keb went quiet and spent a moment looking at the floor before saying, "I guess I made a math error." He then pulled fifteen dollars out of his pocket and placed it with the rest of Tanner's belongings.

Timber whispered quietly, "Yeah, lots of people have trouble with math. It's a good thing you caught your error. I'd hate to have to tell your customers how bad you are at math and that you might have been accidentally cheating them."

"Don't go there, please. A fellow can get killed around here for simply being too slow supplying service. They'd line up to cut off chunks of me if a rumor ever got started that I cheated them."

"Relax, your secret is safe with me for now," Timber told him, then in the next breath asked, "What can you tell me about Mr. Rogers?"

"Look, young man," Keb began, "I dislike him as much as the next man in this town, but I don't have a death wish." Keb looked at the front and then the rear door before continuing, "Talking about them gets people killed. So, if you don't mind, we'll talk about the weather. That's still a safe subject, at least until they figure out a way to control that, too." Keb looked at the front and back doors again.

None of this was lost on Timber. He'd seen this before—towns under siege by greedy, violent men who will stop at nothing to get rich or become richer. The list of their crimes was as long as a man's arm. They were as dangerous as a grizzly bear in heat.

"I can't help but wonder why anyone built a town way out here in the high desert. The soil isn't suitable for farming, there's no lumber for harvesting, and no surface water to speak of. So, what's the attraction?" Timber asked.

"Young man, there you go again," Keb said.

"What? You can't talk about why your town was founded?"

"I'm sure you're smart enough to figure out why towns like this get started. Mining is a major industry in the territory. There have been dozens of towns that have been started only to find the mineral they were after wasn't quite as plentiful as they had thought and others that have turned into bonanzas for the claim holder. Though that isn't what's happening here, mind you. That, I don't want to talk about." Keb turned and walked down the bar, wiping the countertop as he went. Halfway down he stopped and looked at Timber. "Maybe you should go across the street and talk to Zeb. He's about the only one in town who might talk. Though, if he's smart, he'll keep his mouth shut, too." He went back to wiping down the bar, and Timber left the saloon.

## *CHAPTER SIX*

Timber found himself a spot to sit in front of Zeb's saloon and watched the townsfolk as they went about their business. He was surprised at the number of people who lived here, especially the number of children… children.

As he watched the people moving about town, he couldn't help but think about his own child. He'd lost her that fateful night seven years ago. The night that changed everything. It was the night the blinders had been removed from his eyes, and he saw the real world for the first time. It was a world not filled with justice, but corrupted by greed, money and power. A world where being a good man had a double meaning, and it wasn't enough to be honest, brave and true. It meant having a blind spot in your vision where you would allow the rich and powerful to reside, immune from the burdensome laws and morals the rest of mankind had to endure. Where an eye for eye was meant for the lesser man, with the rich and powerful deciding how much justice you were entitled to.

He had been working late that night patrolling the saloon district of town that was overrun by cowpokes fresh off the trail, blowing off steam. Unbeknownst to him, part of the ruckus crowd included the son of the territory's representative in Washington. He had accompanied the cattle drive of his father's herd to be able to say he was an authentic cowboy when he ran for office in a few years. It was all part of a carefully orchestrated plan devised by his father to one day make his son president.

Timber remembered encountering the young man in the alley outside the saloon where he was busy trying to convince one of the saloon girls to have sex. Timber came across them just as she was refusing, and the young man began slapping her around. He was yelling at her, bragging about who he was and because of his status, she had no choice but to do as he ordered or else.

Timber put a gun to his head and explained that because of who *he* was, the sheriff, the young man had no choice but to do as he was ordered. The young man became enraged and tried to attack him, but Timber knocked him out cold and dragged him off to jail. He then returned to patrolling the saloon district.

While he was out on patrol, someone had gone into the jail and released the "would-be" president and rapist. Timber didn't know who it was, but he was determined to find out.

The other deputies on duty continued to round up the drunks all night long without anyone noticing that one prisoner had disappeared. In fact, it was customary to place the drunks in the cells and sort out who was who the next day after they had slept it off.

Timber discovered the would-be rapist wasn't there when they got around to sorting out the drunks the next day. He wasn't happy, but he was unable to discover how the man had gotten away or even who he was.

That night, Timber was on duty yet again and, as usual, there were plenty of drunks to deal with. The real problems began around two in the morning. As Timber entered the saloon, he heard a woman screaming. He immediately started across the room but was cut off by some drunk cowboys and was forced to shove them out of the way. When he reached the stairs, there were five men blocking his way.

"Make way, gentlemen! I'm needed upstairs!" he yelled. The men looked at him and sneered. "Let's not do this right now, boys. Can't you hear the woman screaming?" Timber asked.

One of the men, standing front and center, was dressed in black and wearing a pair of pearl handled six-shooters. "I don't hear nothing, and you ain't getting upstairs anytime soon," he said.

"What? Why?" Timber asked.

"Does it really matter? Isn't it enough to know you ain't getting up there until I say so?"

"Don't make this into a problem for yourself. By interfering with me, you're becoming an accomplice. You'll get the same time in jail or the quick death at the end of a rope, same as the man who did it. Are you prepared to deal with those consequences?" Timber asked him.

"Go away, sheriff man, or I might just have to shoot you so I can get back to my drinking," the man threatened.

"Then I guess you'd better make your move, because I'm coming through," Timber yelled.

The man drew his guns and although he was fast, he wasn't as fast as Timber. Timber shot him dead along with two of the four other men who had tried to come to the man's defense. The remaining two men held up their hands and stepped aside. The gunshots had quieted the whole saloon, and the woman's voice suddenly sounded very loud.

Timber raced up the stairs. As he reached the top, the screaming abruptly stopped. He hesitated in the sudden silence, not sure which way to go. A saloon girl, standing in the hallway, discreetly pointed to the left. Timber raced left, only to find himself tackled by a large man dressed in black. It was a short battle, ending with Timber pistol-whipping his attacker and moving on down the hallway. Three doors down, Timber saw a gun in the crack of the door. He didn't hesitate, firing his gun at the door and killing the man behind it. When he reached the seventh and final door, he raced up and crashed right through it.

As he entered the room, Timber was pummeled by something solid on the back of his head, and he went down hard. He was lying there, unable to get up or see clearly, when a face he recognized came into view. It was the young man from the night before. He stood there with a very unhappy look, his face streaked with blood. He was wiping blood off his hands with a rag of some sort.

"You are a real pain in my rear end, Sheriff. This is twice in two nights that you've interrupted my pleasure. I think I shall make an example of you. You'll be a good lesson for others regarding what you shouldn't do when dealing with the upper class. You see, Sheriff, the rules don't apply to us. I thought that would have been made apparent to you last night, when I simply walked out of your pathetic little jail, though I can see now you are rather thickheaded. That little rap on the head with a lead pipe would have killed most men, but not you. Oh, no, not you. In fact, you're not even knocked out, although I bet it does hurt quite a bit.

"So, what can I do that will make a lasting impression upon you? Something that will truly sink in through that thick skull of yours. Oh, I know—I've heard you're a married man with a small child. I'll make a special trip to your home and give your wife and child the attention they deserve. Perhaps then you'll keep your nose out of other people's business." The young man stood smirking at him for several seconds then stepped away.

Timber was still so woozy he couldn't get up, but he could roll over. When he did so, the room spun, and he blacked out for what he thought was a moment but must have been considerably longer. When he finally opened his eyes again, he saw two of his deputies standing over him. Out in the hallway, there was a man leaning against the wall throwing up.

"What… what… what happened?" Timber mumbled, and his deputies leaned down and told him to lie still, the doc was coming. Then he remembered… the young man said he was going to go after his wife and daughter.

"Help me up," Timber said as he tried to sit up. "Help me up," he said again. The deputies grabbed his arms and pulled him to his feet. They held on to him for several seconds, waiting for him to get his balance. When the dizziness passed, Timber looked to his side and saw the saloon girl from the night before. She was naked and tied spread eagle on the bed. Large areas of her skin had been cut away. A large cross had been carved on her abdomen. It was a horrific sight. Blood was splattered everywhere. The worst thing was her nose had been cut off and her eyes cut out. Timber looked away, fighting back the urge to vomit, and pushed away from his deputies.

"I need your help. The man who did this said he was going to go after my wife and daughter. Let's go. I need to get to them," Timber pleaded.

"Good afternoon, Mr. Timber." Timber heard the voice and tried to find his deputies, but they no longer existed. He opened his eyes slightly and saw he was sitting on a porch in front of a saloon in a town he was barely familiar with.

"Good afternoon, Mr. Timber." Timber heard the greeting again, and this time he opened his eyes completely. There before him stood Mr. Castleman.

## *CHAPTER SEVEN*

"I see you're hard at work dealing with those stressful issues that required you to wait until this afternoon to meet with my client," Castleman said sarcastically.

"Actually, I made fair progress on that front. It's an occupational hazard, the body requiring the occasional power nap." Timber could be sarcastic, too.

"So, have you made sufficient progress to ride with me back to my client's ranch?" Castleman asked, his tone more demanding than questioning.

"I haven't quite reached my quota for the day yet, but perhaps you might be able to help," Timber suggested.

"Really, Mr. Timber. I was only obliged to intervene with Tanner because it was in my client's best interests. I seriously doubt I can provide you with any further assistance."

Timber pulled some papers from his pocket. "Does this man work for Rogers?" He handed him one of the wanted posters, and Castleman glanced at it. Timber could see he knew the man, but was doing his best to conceal it.

"I don't get involved with the personnel, Mr. Timber."

"Well, how about these men?" Timber handed him three more wanted posters and watched Castleman's reaction again. With each picture, Castleman's face gave him away despite his continued lies of not knowing the people Mr. Rogers employed. Timber next handed him the wanted poster for a man he had killed a week ago. Again, Castleman had no reaction, confirming he was lying about not knowing the others.

"Okay, then, I think that wraps up working for the day. I guess if you still want company on the trip, I could tear myself away."

"It would please Mr. Rogers to have the meeting as soon as possible," Castleman replied.

They retrieved their horses from the livery and road southwest. Shortly thereafter, the trail swung east and then south between two large rock outcroppings. Strangely, Castleman had said absolutely nothing up to this point. Timber was dying to know any number of things about Mr. Rogers. He decided to try and see if he could garner any information from Castleman.

"So, why so far out of town?" Timber asked.

"Mr. Rogers likes to be near his business," Castleman replied.

"What exactly does he mine?"

Castleman's face tightened, which meant he was thinking of a lie to tell. "Mr. Rogers' companies mine several minerals," he replied but didn't say which ones.

"I haven't seen any wagon trains taking the minerals out. How does he ship them?" Timber asked.

"We're between shipments," Castleman lied.

"Oh, I see. There's not another route, is there?" Timber watched as Castleman's face tightened again, but he said nothing. Timber let him off the hook, since it would just be a lie anyway. "Yeah, stockpiling until there's enough to send... Smart." Timber decided to play as dumb as Castleman thought he was. "So, how many wagons do you send out at a time?"

"Oh, between twenty and twenty-five."

"Really? Why so few? I'd have thought with Rogers being such a rich man, his wagon trains would be at least a hundred wagons long."

Castleman got all huffy. "That's *Mister* Rogers to you. I let it go earlier, but I must insist that you address him as his station in life dictates your respect."

"My mistake. I'll try to remember to include the mister part," Timber told him, just to avoid any arguments. Fact is, he'd still call him Rogers until he earned his respect.

"You'll fare a whole lot better if you treat people with the proper respect," Castleman lectured.

"I'll try to remember that. So, how many men work for Mr. Rogers?" Timber tried to bring the conversation back on track.

"I'm afraid you'll have to ask Mr. Rogers questions of that nature. I'm not at liberty to discuss my client's affairs." Castleman used his position to not only sidestep the question, but to kill the conversation. They rode the rest of the way in silence.

Rogers' ranch consisted of a huge house built in a U-shape, three stories tall. The house itself was surrounded by a two-story wall that was six feet thick. There were gates on both the front and back sides. The house and wall were made of adobe bricks covered with stucco and painted white. The house had a red tile roof. In addition, there was a large barn, stables, a bunk house half the size of the main house and several smaller buildings over near the mine, maybe two miles away. Next to those buildings was a large hole in the mountain that Timber assumed was the mine.

Castleman led him into the inner courtyard of the main house where they were greeted by Mr. Rogers at the front door. Rogers was nothing like Timber had imagined. Instead of being a large, strapping man, he was small and wiry. He wore glasses and had thinning, gray hair. He was dressed in a gray business suit and was smoking a cigar.

"Good afternoon, Mr. Timber," Mr. Rogers shouted with a smile on his face as they rode up.

"Afternoon," Timber replied.

"I see Mr. Castleman has been persuasive, as usual. I hope he wasn't too heavy-handed in getting you to agree to meet with me," he said, still smiling.

"If he had been, I'd have just shot him," Timber replied, smiling widely.

Mr. Rogers was taken aback by Timber's off-color comment and hesitated a moment before continuing. "Well, perhaps you'll be able to extend me the same courtesy. Now, come in and let's have something to drink in my office," Mr. Rogers turned around to lead the way. Castleman stepped up to Rogers and whispered in his ear. Rogers cocked his head slightly at the message.

Once they had reached Mr. Rogers' office, a maid pushed a cart into the room with a pitcher of beer, a fifth of whiskey and a pot of coffee on it. Timber accepted a beer and took a seat by the window.

"It's quite a spread you have here," Timber said as he admired the view.

"Thank you, but we're not here to talk about my ranch, Mr. Timber. We're here to talk about you. Your future. I understand that last night you were forced to kill four men in

Zeb's saloon, and that it was a remarkable display of shooting skills that few have ever seen. I have need of a man with those skills, and I'll pay top dollar for him."

"I already have a job," Timber replied.

"Yes, as a bounty hunter. If you had managed to keep the four bodies, you would have had a sizeable payday. But someone managed to steal them from the undertaker. It's too bad you can't get someone who is a known public figure to attest to the fact you did indeed kill them, and that the bodies have been buried here. I believe Mr. Castleman could fashion such a document, and you could then wire the capital for your money. I know a number of individuals in the capital, including the territorial governor. I'm sure between us, we could make sure you'd be paid," Mr. Rogers offered.

"That would make things so much easier. However, I doubt they'd make an exception for me just so I could take another job. I'm not exactly a well-known bounty hunter. I'm just one of perhaps as many as three dozen, maybe more." Timber tried to side-step his suggestion.

"Don't worry about it. We'll make the arrangements, plus we'll make sure that the necessary people here sign off on your letter," Mr. Rogers assured Timber.

"What exactly would this job entail?" Timber asked.

"The job would be to guard my shipments. We've been having trouble shipping out the minerals without robbers staging attacks on the wagon trains," Mr. Rogers explained.

"Isn't that simply solved by adding more guards?"

"It would, if I could be sure the men I hired were not already working for Winters."

"What does Winters have to do with it?"

"I can't confirm it, but I strongly believe that Winters runs the gangs that have been attacking my wagon trains. The losses have not yet been of a level that has forced me out of business, but I fear the day is coming when they will get an entire wagon train," Rogers explained.

"I see. What are you doing now for security?" Timber asked, honestly wanting to help Rogers get a handle on the problem.

"I'm afraid that is not open for discussion until you're actually an employee, Mr. Timber."

"I understand. I'm afraid, though, that I'm not the man for you. I might be able to recommend a couple of men to you, but it's not a good fit for me."

"How can you say no, when you don't know what the job pays?" Rogers snapped.

"It's not a question of pay. It's a question of temperament, and a job like that doesn't fit my temperament," Timber replied.

Rogers suddenly took on a more sinister demeanor. "What is your real purpose for being here? I know Winters has been talking to you. Do you work for him? Did he put you up to seeing me?"

"What are you talking about? You asked me to meet with you. You sent Castleman here to fetch me. But, just so your mind is at ease, I turned down the job Winters offered. I have a job, and I like it. So, I'll be going now. It was good to meet you and good luck. If you want the names of a couple of men who might be interested, let me know," Timber said as he got up and walked out.

While riding back to town, Timber couldn't help but wonder how this little turf war was being waged. He'd have to do a little more investigating before deciding how to proceed with his job. It might not be as bad here as it first appeared. Maybe Winters was the only problem. After all, he practically admitted he was robbing Rogers' shipments. Then again, both of them were charging protection money, and both were hiring criminals and wanted men.

## CHAPTER EIGHT

"Well, what exactly did you learn about Mr. Timber?" Mr. Rogers asked Castleman now that they were alone.

"He's a bounty hunter with a territorial mandate that gives him extreme latitude in dealing with criminals and wanted men. He's been charged with the elimination of men who are wanted and/or are criminals. There will be no court hearings for the men he collects. He's charged with simply killing them in any manner he deems efficient."

"What? What happened to being innocent until proven guilty?" Mr. Rogers practically shouted.

"That's no longer in effect in our territory. The territorial governor secretly signed an order appointing Timber to comb the territory for wanted men and kill them. All men currently wanted for any crime are to be considered armed and dangerous, thus all of them have had their status changed to 'Wanted: Dead or Alive,' with the emphasis on dead," Mr. Castleman explained.

"How can they get away with this? Timber could be out settling old scores. What was he before he was appointed executioner?" Mr. Rogers inquired.

"He was a prisoner at Great Falls Penitentiary. But before that, he was a sheriff. A very good sheriff. The story is that he was trying to stop Wilbur Gentry's son from committing a rape and the murder of a saloon girl–"

"Wait, the son of THE Wilbur Gentry? The Wilbur Gentry who is one of the richest men in the world and sets the cattle prices not only for our country, but for all of the western hemisphere? The Wilbur Gentry who is the territory's representative in Washington and has the president's ear?"

"Yes, sir, one and the same," Castleman confirmed, continuing, "Timber tries to stop Wilbur Gentry's son from committing rape, torture and murder, but Cain, Gentry's son, and his bodyguards were able to surprise Timber and knock him out cold. With Timber out of commission, Cain murdered the saloon girl and then went after Timber's wife and daughter to teach him a lesson about minding his own business. Timber recovered and went after Cain. He caught up with him just as Cain finished killing his wife and daughter. Timber killed the four bodyguards and then killed Cain by burning the house to the ground with Cain trapped inside. Eyewitness testimony claims that Timber broke Cain's back and then beat him to a bloody pulp. When his own deputies tried to save Cain, Timber pulled his gun on them and kept them from saving him. There's a persistent rumor, though, that two of Timber's deputies managed to sneak into the house from the other side and save Cain.

"The next day, Timber left for the territorial capital to hunt down Wilbur Gentry himself. He said there was no way that Gentry couldn't have known what his son was doing. He pointed out the bodyguards who stood by and let Cain murder the saloon girl and then his wife and daughter.

"What Timber hadn't counted on was the fact that Wilbur Gentry had the whole territory in his pocket, and when he heard that Timber had murdered his son, he became enraged. Gentry sent ten men to kill Timber, but they failed. Timber killed them all and managed to get to the Gentry ranch, and inside the ranch house itself, before the U.S. Marshals managed to subdue Timber. It was all in vain, too. Gentry had left the territory the day before and wasn't even home.

"They held a trial in secret. The territory's top three judges decided there were extenuating circumstances and refused to hang him, which hasn't made them friends of Gentry's. In fact, they gave the man life with a chance for parole in twenty-five years. Then the territorial governor, a personal friend of Gentry's, was caught stealing from the territory's treasury, and a new governor came to power. He pardoned Timber, provided he used his unique talents with a gun to hunt down the criminals and wanted men in the territory. That way, when the territory asked for statehood, they would look that much better by having crime under control," Mr. Castleman concluded.

"So, where does this leave us? He will surely decide what we do is criminal in nature," Mr. Rogers bemoaned.

"He's already aware of the fee we're charging local businesses in order to have your men frequent their establishments. Keb was less than silent when Timber first entered his saloon."

"And what about Tanner?" Mr. Rogers then asked.

"I had the judge write a release order. He should have been released by now. I suspect he'll spend the afternoon explaining to Keb how you would prefer that no one talks about your business with anyone, not even among themselves," Castleman assured him.

"That's all well and good, but what about Timber?"

"Tanner and his men have been instructed to do their best to eliminate Mr. Timber, and I believe they will try to do so this very evening. I've sent ten men to help. Timber will not escape them. I've also taken the liberty, and the precaution, of informing Winters we'll be in town tonight in force, so he and his men should stay clear to avoid any unwanted bloodshed. I also told him we're not interested in any conflict with him this evening, but there will be more than sufficient manpower to deal with him if the need arises."

"That's good, very good. But make sure we have sufficient manpower here tonight, as well. I wouldn't put it past Winters to stage an attack here, thinking he could take it easily, since we'll have so many men in town tonight," Mr. Rogers directed.

"I have already armed the men working the mine and told everyone they will be on duty all night tonight," Castleman said.

****

Arriving back in town, Timber went directly to the jail to check on his prisoner. What he found when he arrived did not make him happy.

"Evening, Sheriff. How's my prisoner doing?" Timber asked as he stepped through the door.

Without looking up from his newspaper, the sheriff stated, "He's gone."

"What? He escaped? How'd that happen?!" Timber bellowed.

"He was released," the sheriff explained without elaboration.

"On whose authority? I take it you don't remember what I told you when we met!" Timber yelled as he leaned over the sheriff's desk.

"It's all here in the court order," the sheriff said calmly as he shoved the paper towards him.

It was a telegram ordering the immediate release of Thomas Tanner into the custody of one Harold J. Castleman, and stated, "The defendant is hereby reprimanded to come before the court on its next scheduled visit to Heaven Brook." It was signed by the Honorable Territorial Judge, Winston T. Klineman.

"Klineman doesn't have any jurisdiction in this case!" Timber yelled.

"Well, obviously Klineman thinks he does, and I am subject to his rulings. So, I guess if you want the order lifted, you'll have to find a judge who will override him." The sheriff smirked at Timber.

Timber almost lost it, but at the last moment, he reeled himself back in. The sheriff wasn't going anywhere. He'd deal with him when the big fish had been dealt with. Timber stomped out of the jailhouse without saying another word.

He marched right down to the telegraph office and sent a telegram to the judge he answered to, asking for his help in reining in Judge Klineman who was helping the criminals here in Heaven Brook. He asked that he send an overriding order as soon as possible and left it to the judge to solve.

## *CHAPTER NINE*

Timber headed for Keb's saloon to make sure he hadn't been attacked by Tanner when he got out. Timber entered the saloon but found it empty. There wasn't a single soul in there, even though it was going on seven in the evening. He knew right then that something was wrong.

"Keb, you around?" Timber called out. No response. Cautiously, he moved slowly through the saloon, his hand hovering over his gun. When he reached the end of the bar he looked behind it, but no one was there. He moved towards the rear of the saloon's tent where it joined to another tent that served as the saloon's storage area and probably Keb's residence.

The two spaces were separated by a heavy canvas flap that didn't let any light through. Slowly, Timber pushed back the fabric and stepped through. The space was dark, unlike the well-lit saloon, so Timber was forced to find a lantern. There was one sitting behind the flap. He lit it and began searching through the space, the lantern lighting the way. Keb wasn't in the storage area, either, leaving his quarters as the only place he could be if he were here. Timber called out his name and pushed through the heavy canvas flap divider between the storage area and Keb's residence. He held the lantern out in front of him.

Keb's quarters were modest. He had an old rocking chair, a bed in the corner and a table with two chairs. There was one chest of drawers and an old wood slat chest with ornate tin straps wrapped around it. In the center of the space was a large potbelly stove.

Keb was lying on the floor behind the potbelly stove facedown, a small pool of blood around his head. Seeing the old man lying on the floor, Timber hastened his stride and bent down to aid Keb. His first touch of the old man's body told him there was nothing he could do.

Keb was stone cold. As Timber began to stand up, he heard something move behind him and started to turn around, but he never got that far. Tanner had snuck up on him while he was busy searching for Keb. He delivered a blow to the back of Timber's head with a wooden axe handle, and he went down hard. Tanner stepped up closely and stared down at Timber.

"I told you I'd be back, and now you're mine to do with as I see fit. You're going to regret the day you crossed my path, Timber. We're going to beat you to death," Tanner threatened as he grabbed Timber's gun and tossed it across the space. As he did so, five more men stepped from the shadows and yanked Timber off the floor.

Despite being semi-conscious, Timber knew he had to fight to live and began struggling with the two men who were holding him up. He managed to break one arm free and deliver one blow to the man holding the opposite arm, knocking that man senseless. That was when Timber was overwhelmed. Fists seemed to rain down on him from every direction. He felt them all, but only for a moment. After that, his body started shutting down. Propped up by one or more men, other men delivered blows to his face and body. If he tried to wrench himself away, someone would punch him in the kidneys as hard as they could. Timber lasted for maybe ten minutes as a human punching bag before he passed out, and they suddenly stopped.

They threw water in his face to try and rouse him. They wanted him to see and feel every blow. But just when Timber regained semi-consciousness, he was dropped on the floor and kicked several times as his attackers left the room.

Moments after being left to die, Timber heard loud shouting and then gunfire erupted in the distance. Timber was unaware that Winters' men were attacking, and now a town-wide gunfight was underway. Winters' men were treating this as an all-out war and were attacking Rogers' ranch, as well.

They dynamited the mine entrance, leaving over a hundred men sealed inside. The battle for the ranch house didn't go as easily for Winters' men. It seemed Rogers' men had planted nitroglycerin in small, shallow holes as land mines. More than three dozen of Winters' men were killed by the mines and another two dozen were shot and killed by snipers hidden on the second and third stories of the house and the roof. Winters' men finally retreated into the night, and the attack at the ranch was over.

Back in town, the firefight raged up and down the main street and in the back alleys. The locals who didn't work directly for either power broker hid in their residences or climbed aboard their buckboards, riding a few miles out of town to spend the night in the open despite the cool weather.

After losing half their number, Winters' men finally retreated from the ranch. Rogers' men hadn't fared much better, but they still held all the high ground, the rooftop of Rogers' home and the top of the two-story compound wall, despite Winters' men outnumbering them. They had made a substantial number of kills.

When Rogers' men pulled back, Winters' men went in search of Timber. They had last seen him entering the saloon. Upon searching the saloon, they could only find Keb's body and a good deal of blood. They figured Timber had been beaten to death after finding the bloody axe handle laying on the floor.

They searched the town for two hours. They beat up several citizens simply because they needed to work off their frustration when they were unable to find Timber. No one had paid any attention to the undertaker that night, but he had paid attention to what was going on. He had seen Timber go into Keb's saloon after Tanner and five other men went in an hour earlier. He saw them leave a half-hour later when the shooting broke out. During the gun battle, his curiosity got the better of him, and he decided to go check on Keb and Timber. He found Zeb in the saloon, and together they searched for the two men. They found them in the residence, both badly beaten. Keb sadly had been beaten to death, but Timber was still hanging in there, though barely alive. Zeb and the undertaker dragged Timber out of Keb's residence and over to the undertaker's workyard.

The undertaker went about his business that night as usual, collecting the dead. He acted as though Timber was just another body. By the time the men from Winters' gang had gotten around to searching his place of business, the undertaker had more than four dozen bodies piled up in his wagon. He'd have to bury them within the next two days or risk bringing cholera to the town. Winters' men gave the bodies a quick, cursory inspection before concluding Rogers' men must have helped Timber escape.

An hour later, Timber was packed in a coffin, loaded onto another wagon, then hauled out of town as though to be buried along with the other bodies. At first light, the coffin in which Timber was hidden was opened, and he was lifted out. He was then taken into a cave where he was laid on a makeshift bed, and a man began treating his injuries.

## *CHAPTER TEN*

"Oh, good, you're awake. That's a good sign. I can't be sure, but I believe you have suffered a good number of internal injuries. I'd say you have several broken ribs, a bruised spleen, broken nose and cheekbone. Based on the large lump on the back of your head, I strongly believe you have suffered a concussion as well. You've lost a few teeth, I've had to give you several dozen stitches, and you'll need to stay in bed for several days. Do you like to read? If so, I can bring you several books I found entertaining to help pass the time."

"Who are you, and where am I?" Timber asked in a low whisper. Breathing was a difficult task.

"Oh, please excuse me. I forgot you're a stranger to our town. I'm Dr. Brown, but most people just call me Doc. You're in a cave about three miles from the mines," the man told him.

"How did I get here?"

"You have the undertaker and Zeb to thank for that. They dragged you out of Keb's saloon and hid you among the dead, then spirited you out of town with the first lot to be buried," Doc explained.

"What bodies?" Timber asked, confused.

"You were out of it, but in a way, Mr. Winters saved your life. His men attacked Mr. Rogers' men who came to town specifically to kill you. It seems they don't like the idea of a bounty hunter collecting their men," the doctor said with a grin, then added, "but the rest of us are grateful as hell you're here, and we'd like to try and help you if we can. Especially now that so many on both sides have been killed."

"How long have I been here?"

"Just overnight, but you're in no condition to move let alone get involved with the forty or more gunfighters still remaining on both sides."

"My gun?" Timber asked.

"We haven't found your gun just yet, but we have left you several handguns and lots of ammo under the bed. We'll be checking on you a few times each day until you're well enough to get on a horse. Then we hope you'll be able to help us get rid of these men once and for all. That is, if it doesn't take too long for you to recover. I'm sure they're busy recruiting already for a second round," the doctor informed him.

"A few minutes ago, you said, from 'the mines'... I thought there was only one mine," Timber said, trying to get clarification from the doctor.

"Oh, no, there are two mines. One belongs to Winters and the other to Rogers. Each one produces on and off, usually in extraordinary amounts, and then it stops. They have to expend large sums of money to get more gold. During the digging periods, the mining concern that isn't seeing large amounts of gold from their efforts goes on raiding parties against the other mine. Plus, they've used their gold to buy the mortgages of the other property owners and forced them to make them partners, usually fifty/fifty. Those who own their property outright do all they can to limit their business, otherwise they pay them at least thirty percent of their profits. If they pay Winters and Rogers, they encourage their employees to use their businesses to enrich their take." The doctor explained the whole corrupt system to Timber, leaving it in his hands to decide the best course of action to eliminate the corruption.

Timber's recovery took longer than the doctor had hoped. His ribs were in the worse shape. After a week of rest, he still couldn't raise his arms. Every day when either Doc, the undertaker or Zeb stopped in, Timber was given an update regarding what had happened in the last twenty-four hours. Apparently, both sides had had enough of killing for the moment as they were busy recruiting new gunhands and preparing for an all-out war.

After ten days, Timber forced himself to start practicing shooting. It hurt, and his aim was rotten, but by the fourth day of practice he felt he was well on his way to recovery, at least with regards shooting. On the fifteenth day, Zeb brought him his own gun that had finally been found, and then he really began practicing.

****

"So, where the hell is he!" Mr. Rogers shouted at Mr. Castleman.

"He could be anywhere or nowhere. I suggested we have the doctor and the undertaker followed a week ago, but you refused to do so. You were afraid it was too risky, and we couldn't afford to take even a minor amount of manpower away from the mine." Mr. Castleman assessed the blame where it belonged.

Rogers stood staring at Castleman for several seconds before he issued a new directive. "Send four men to interrogate the doctor, but don't rough him up too much. We need his skills, but they can mess up Zeb, the saloonkeeper, all they want. The same goes for the undertaker."

"Now we'll make some progress. You watch and see," Mr. Castleman said smugly.

The four men arrived in town just as the doc had finished making a house call on one of the wounded men from the gunfight. He was tired and in no mood to be quizzed by Rogers' goons.

"Afternoon, Doc," a big man dressed in dirty clothes with a beard and long, dirty, stringy hair said as the doc stepped into his office.

He had locked the door when he left, and the four men sitting on his nice, clean furniture in clothes that looked as though they had last been washed in a muddy puddle, had to have broken in. "What do you think you're doing? That door was locked, and you have no business in here when I'm not here!" Doc shouted.

"Relax, Doc. We didn't steal anything—yet. We're only here to ask you a few questions," the big man said as he sneered at the doctor.

"Like what? Can't you see I'm extremely busy, no thanks to you."

"Have you treated the stranger called Timber?" the big man asked as he stared at the doctor.

"No, I haven't. Why? Is he injured?" asked the doctor, keeping a straight face.

"Do you know if anyone is helping him?"

"Not that I'm aware of. And even if I did, I wouldn't tell you," the doctor replied curtly.

"Have you seen him around anywhere?" The big man reached out and knocked over the doctor's microscope. "Oops, sorry, Doc," the big man apologized insincerely.

"Get out! Get out! If you don't leave now, I won't treat you for anything," the doctor bellowed.

"Now don't get all excited, Doc. We'll go, just as soon as you tell us when you last saw him," the big man calmly stated as he knocked a jar of pills off a shelf, shattering the jar on the floor.

"The last I saw him, he was being dragged away by some of Winters' men the night of the big gunfight. Now get the hell out of my office!" the doctor screamed at the four men who slowly stood and filed out the door.

The big man brought up the rear, and as he reached to close the door, he leaned back in and said, "Don't even think about not treating us, Doc. If you don't, you'll need a doctor yourself. Real bad." Then he was gone.

The doctor slowly sank into a nearby chair to catch his breath. Within seconds, he knew he had to warn the others about these men asking questions, including exactly what he had told them.

Two hours later, the doctor was at the cave where Timber was recovering and told him everything that had happened. The doctor was very apologetic, but Timber explained that it was for the best, because it gave him an idea.

"Doc, go back into town and tell Zeb and the undertaker to tell Winters' men when they come by asking questions, that they saw Rogers' men drag me away. Feed misinformation to both sides. Then, I need you to get me a case of dynamite. I've some seeds of discontent to plant so neither side thinks they can wait any longer to attack. Be sure every able-bodied man you can trust not to talk to Winters, Rogers or the sheriff gets a shotgun and plenty of shells. If I can pull this off, we'll have both parties on Main Street, where we can end this corruption once and for all. But everyone will have to shoot a bad man or two. There's no other way."

The doctor promised to get at least twenty men, and he'd await further instruction from Timber as to where and how to use them best.

When the doctor returned this time, he found Winters' men in his office wanting to know the exact same things that Rogers' men had. The doctor fed them the story Timber had concocted, and they left as happy as larks to convey the story.

Zeb and the undertaker didn't have as easy a time convincing the men from both camps of the story. Zeb got knocked around quite a bit by Rogers' men before they accepted that Winters' men had dragged Timber away. The undertaker also got beat up, but it was Winters' men who got to him first. They left only after having destroyed several coffins he had just finished making. When Rogers' men came to see him, they accepted the story about Winters' men dragging him off, but still inflicted a minimal amount of pain to him just to be sure.

That night, despite being quite sore, Zeb managed to bring the case of dynamite out to Timber, and he suggested that Timber move right away. He told him about an old cabin a few miles out of town to the east, back up in the rocks. It was old, and few knew it was there. Zeb was afraid that either—or both—Winters and Rogers had men following him and the others in their efforts to find him. Timber agreed to leave and told Zeb not to come back or look for him. He'd take care of himself from now on.

Timber left the cave within ten minutes of Zeb leaving. He followed the trail left by Zeb after sweeping down the cave, so it appeared to be unused. He left two holsters with six-guns in them and several empty ammo boxes, so if there was someone watching Zeb, they might assume Zeb was trying to learn how to shoot. Hopefully, it wouldn't cause him any additional injuries at the hands of those murderous thugs.

## *CHAPTER ELEVEN*

"I tend to believe them, sir. We beat up the undertaker and Zeb pretty good before they gave up what they saw, confirming what the doctor had told us," the big man informed Mr. Rogers and Mr. Castleman.

"How exactly did the doctor come to share what he saw again?" Mr. Rogers asked as he shared a look with Mr. Castleman.

"It was like you said. We weren't to beat up the doc. We just stood there staring at him and not saying a word. We were trying to intimidate him. I finally told him we'd go away if he answered our questions. He did, but I could tell he was holding something back. So, I accidentally pushed over his microscope. He got real pissy with me, so I knocked a bottle of pills off the shelf and asked the question again. He wanted to know if he told me would we leave right away. I said sure thing. That's when he told us that Winters' men took him. He was real scared by that time, and he was real concerned about me breaking things so, no, I don't think he lied." The big man struggled, breathless from having to talk so long.

"And what about Zeb? When did he tell you?" Mr. Castleman inquired.

"Well, old Zeb, he wasn't very friendly or talkative. We had to force the conversation with him, and by the time we finished with him, he was offering to share anything we wanted to know. It was when I broke his nose after asking him for the third or fourth time what he knew about the stranger, that he told us. Of course, we had to continue to beat him for a few minutes and then asked him again to be sure he wasn't lying. He answered the questions pretty much as he had the first time."

"And the undertaker?" Mr. Castleman asked.

"It was easiest with him. Winters' men had just left when we got there, and they had worked him over pretty good. He said it was because they wanted to make sure he didn't tell anyone what he saw the night of the big gunfight. He then told us he saw Winters' men drag Timber away. He had no idea why they did it, but they did, and if they've killed him, they also buried him."

"Okay, that'll be all." Mr. Rogers dismissed the big man and then turned to Mr. Castleman. "Why would they help him? What could they possibly gain?" Mr. Rogers pondered.

"I think they helped him in an effort to curry favor with Mr. Timber. After all, they're as much in his crosshairs as we are. But if he were to feel grateful to them for having saved his life, perhaps they think he'll give them a chance to change or leave instead of just killing them on sight," Mr. Castleman stated.

"Okay, then we'll have to move as soon as we have enough men. We'll attack their compound in town in full force. We'll kill two birds with one stone, both Winters and Timber," Mr. Rogers stated.

****

"They're not lying, boss." One of the man mountains Winters employed was explaining what he had found out about Timber's whereabouts. "I'd bet the house on that. We beat the undertaker almost senseless to get him to talk, then we found Zeb lying on the floor. Rogers' men had just been there, and they had beat him pretty badly. He gave it up with just a little pressure. Rogers' men had been there because they wanted to make sure he kept his mouth shut about them having taken Timber away. Zeb said they had a use for him, against you, but they didn't say how. The doctor was practically shaking when we surrounded him in the alley behind his office. We shoved him around a bit, but we didn't hurt him too much as you ordered. He said that Rogers' men had been there, and they warned him to keep his mouth shut or else," the man finished.

"I want you to tail the doc and the undertaker, night and day. Also, put a couple of spies on the Rogers' ranch. I want to know the moment Rogers makes a move towards town. We're going to set up one hell of a surprise for him," Mr. Winters informed him. As the man turned to leave, Winters told him to send Bond into see him. Bond arrived a minute later.

"Yes, boss. What can I do for you?" Bond asked.

"I need you to gather a hundred men and at least fifty wagons. Make sure everyone is loaded up. Tomorrow night, when I draw Rogers into town, I want you to go out to his mine and steal fifty wagons full of his stockpiled material. You'll need shovels, masks and guns," he ordered.

"Will do, boss. But won't he already have it loaded in wagons? Wouldn't it make more sense to use his wagons?" Bond questioned.

"Did I ask you what you were thinking?" Mr. Winters snarled.

"No, sir," Bond replied sheepishly.

"Then I suggest you keep your mouth shut. I have a source that tells me Rogers has changed his tactics to try and make it more difficult to steal his takings. So, no, I don't want you stealing empty wagons," Mr. Winters barked. "Now, get busy preparing for the job."

****

Timber watched Rogers' mine and ranch all the next day, and by late afternoon he knew how to best hurt him. He then scouted the Winters' mine and learned the same things. The two places actually operated very similarly. It was those similar procedures that would allow him to put both gangs in very difficult positions that evening. What he had planned wasn't going to be easy, but he could do it. It was all just a matter of timing.

## *CHAPTER TWELVE*

It was now almost a month since the big gunfight, as the townsfolk were calling it, and still the calm aftermath was in place. Each gang added one or two men a day and were close to or slightly more manned than they had been the day of the big gunfight. Rogers had gotten his mine reopened and was reaping the benefits of Winters having set off explosives in the mine shaft opening. To Rogers' surprise, and Winters' chagrin, the explosion that had closed off the entrance had also revealed another vein of gold running just five feet above the existing mine. Rogers had his men start mining it immediately even while the rescue and cleanup continued.

Using the darkness of the moonless night, Timber made his way down to the area where Rogers staged his wagon trains. He found a hundred and fifty wagons staged in three rows of fifty wagons each. He spent the evening cutting the dynamite into quarter sticks with the intention of placing one on each axle of every wagon, which would blow the axles either in half or off the wagon all together. It was a painstaking task, taking four hours to complete.

Timber ran the fuse a hundred feet from the cluster of wagons being careful not to lay it too close to any of the walking paths in and around the wagons. He struck a match and lit the fuse, standing for a brief moment, visualizing the destruction to come, when he realized he was entirely too close. He turned and ran as fast as he could to the rocks another hundred yards beyond where he had been standing. It was painful to say the least. With every step he took, his ribs were jostled, sending shooting pain through his body. Once he made it to the rocks, he remembered he had to climb over the outcropping to get to his horse, which was another torturous activity to endure. He sat there getting his breath, hoping something easier would present itself.

The explosion occurred in stages. Timber had aligned the explosives starting at the far end of the rows with the main fuse running the length of each row of wagons. The wagons exploded one row at a time like a string of firecrackers. Timber was two hundred yards away but was still showered with debris. When it was over, the entire group of wagons were destroyed. He was especially proud of the fact that the remnants had caught fire due to the explosions. Now Rogers was out of business until he could build up his wagon train again.

****

"What the hell?" screamed Mr. Rogers as the vibration from the explosion reached the ranch house, shaking it to its foundations. Mr. Castleman, who had retired to his suite of rooms, was awakened from a sound sleep in the arms of his mistress. He threw on a bathrobe and came running downstairs to the veranda, where Mr. Rogers had already arrived and was watching the flames in the distance.

"What was that? Was it the mine again? What happened?" Castleman shouted as he ran up to Mr. Rogers.

"That son of a bitch has sabotaged me for the last time! Castleman, get all the men up and get them ready to ride. At dawn, we're all going to town and killing that son of a bitch Winters along with all his men. I don't care if we have to burn the town to the ground. We're getting this job done once and for all!

"Does that mean you're going with the men?" Mr. Castleman asked. He wondered whether Rogers had a death wish.

"Damn right, I am, and so are you!" Mr. Rogers shouted again.

"I am not going into a gun battle. I'm a lawyer. What do I know about guns?" Mr. Castleman shouted back.

"You've got eight hours to learn," Mr. Rogers snapped at him, then added, "You're going or you're being buried in the mine at sunrise."

"But I'm a lawyer, not a gunslinger," Mr. Castleman whined.

"Then go pick out the suit you want to buried in!" Mr. Rogers stood there glaring at him.

"I'll send some men to follow the saboteur's trail so we can be sure of who it was before we waste time going into town," Mr. Castleman said resignedly.

"Whatever," Mr. Rogers absently replied. He was once again engrossed in the huge bonfire in the field north of the mine entrance.

Mr. Castleman turned away and climbed the stairs to the second floor where his face broke into a huge grin. Finally, this fool Rogers was going to expose himself, and it was almost a sure thing he would get himself killed. After all, Castleman would be right behind him aiming his gun at his back.

An hour later, shortly after Timber had managed to climb over the rock outcropping, Rogers' men found and followed Timber's footprints to and from the wagon train, then to the rock outcropping. It took another ten minutes to get all the men saddled up before Rogers finally got his men moving, and they followed Timber's trail.

Upon arriving at the compound gate, Timber had mingled with some tracks from other horses and then circled around before doubling back the way he had come in the hopes of losing anyone following him. At the first alleyway, he turned right and headed out of town.

Several of Winters' men watched but didn't open fire per instructions. Winters had sectioned off an area he referred to as the "kill zone." His men were to hold their fire until someone entered that area, hopefully ensuring they remained undiscovered until it was too late.

Timber hightailed it out of town in the direction of Winters' mine. He needed to raise hell with him tonight, as well.

No sooner had he disappeared into the darkness than the men tracking him from Rogers' mine arrived in town. They followed his tracks, stopping a short distance from Winters' gate where they could observe things. They saw that Winters had posted men under the buildings that had line of sight views of the gate and had men lined up along the gate and the wall as if they expected trouble. They snuck back out of town and relayed their findings to Mr. Castleman who would report back to Mr. Rogers.

Timber rode out to the Winters' mine and discovered there weren't very many men working. The mine itself was dark, and there appeared to be just three or four men guarding the entrance. Even the mine office was dark. Winters' wagon train area was a good two hundred yards from the mine entrance but within a few dozen yards of the bunkhouses set in a U-shape beyond the wagon staging area.

The bunkhouses were also dark as though everyone had left or they had all gone to bed early. Timber decided he'd better check out the bunkhouses before moving forward with his plan.

Under cover of darkness on the far side of the bunkhouse, Timber crept up to the building and looked in the windows. The light filtering through the windows on the other end of the building allowed Timber to see the bunks all had lumps in them. There were gun belts and rifles at the foot of each bed. It took ten minutes to confirm that all three bunkhouses were packed with men. All bunks were full and there were dozens of men sleeping on the floor.

He wondered how they were getting into town. There were three bunkhouses, and he guessed they each held at least a hundred men. They might be planning on using the wagons to transport everyone at once. Of course, they could be riding their own horses into town, as well. It occurred to Timber that he needed to warn the townsfolk of the impending war to be fought in their town come tomorrow.

Timber knew what he had to do. He quickly spread out more quarter sticks of dynamite and connected them to the main fuse that he wove throughout the wagons. He placed charges at both ends of the bunkhouses and at the front and back doors. Everything was connected and would explode individually again, just like it had at Rogers' place.

"Hold on there. Who are you?" Timber heard someone say behind him, probably a guard.

"Oh, I'm just out relieving myself. No big deal," Timber said, without looking up or turning around.

"I don't think so. I've worked here for ten years and I can't remember running into you."

"I'm not let out of the mine often. I tend to be anti-social," Timber responded.

"Like I care. Come on, let's go. You've got some explaining to do."

Timber turned around and started to shuffle forward. "I wish you'd just let me alone. I need to get my sleep for tomorrow. Mr. Winters will be quite unhappy if I'm not performing at my best," Timber whined.

"Save your bellyaching for Bond. He'll be the one to decide if you get flogged or not," the guard chuckled. Timber stepped towards the guard with his head down. As he walked past him, Timber threw a punch, hitting him so hard the guard folded up like an accordion. Timber turned and ran, playing out the main fuse as he went. This time, instead of waiting to see what happened, he kept going. Every step sent shooting pain throughout his body. Then, just when he was about to give in and collapse, someone yelled, "Hey, you! Stop!" Thankfully, before the man could draw his gun and fire, the explosions began. The man was close enough to be lifted into the air by the blast's concussion wave, which flung him a good twenty feet before slamming him into the ground.

Timber felt the pressure and some slight heat, but it wasn't enough to slow him down. When he reached the rocks where he had hidden his horse, he looked back and saw not only all three bunkhouses on fire, but the wagons beyond them were burning, as well. To his dismay, he also saw dozens of men silhouetted against the flames wandering about. "Oh, well," Timber said aloud and hoped the ranks had been thinned enough to lessen the impact on the town itself.

With the amount of damage caused at both mines, Timber was confident that both gangs would be at each other's throats by mid-morning. If all went according to plan, by tomorrow night the town of Heaven Brook would be criminal free.

## CHAPTER THIRTEEN

Timber rode back to town via the trail that led past Rogers' mine. Hopefully, the trackers that were sure to have been sent out by Winters would follow the trail here and confirm what they wanted to believe. It would be best for the town if the two gangs expanded the main portion of their forces out here at the mines, thus eliminating the danger the townsfolk would be exposed to. Timber even took an unnecessary risk and rode in quite close to the Rogers ranch house so that the trackers would be sure to reach the conclusion that Rogers was behind the sneak attack. That ruse should solidify Winters attacking Rogers tonight or at first light at the latest. If Timber was right, it would lead Rogers to believe the second attack was a follow-up by Winters. It was all very complicated, and Timber hoped it would work.

From Rogers' place, Timber rode back to town and woke up the telegraph operator to see if he had received any messages in the last few weeks. Sure enough, he had received one from Judge Wellingworth.

*Timber, the second page is your court order for local sheriff to apprehend the criminal he freed. If he refuses, treat as hostile criminal. Take all measures you deem reasonable to apprehend for the two hundred dollar bounty. Consider him another WANTED: DEAD.*

The second page began, *To all parties involved: The court order issued by Judge Klineman is unlawful and hereby rescinded. The local sheriff, one Kevin Nape, is charged with the apprehension of the defendant, one James Tanner. The apprehension is to take place within twenty-four hours of being served with this order. Failure to follow this order will result in the sheriff being labeled a criminal, wanted for aiding and abetting, with a two-hundred-dollar bounty on his head.*

It then provided supporting laws and the territorial governor's signature, as well as Judge Wellingworth's. When Timber presented it to the sheriff, he immediately balked.

"I don't have a death wish. James Tanner is a gunslinger with a truly bad reputation. You're lucky to be alive. If Castleman hadn't reined him in, you'd be dead," the sheriff moaned.

"What, you don't think it could have gone the other way?" Timber grinned.

"I doubt there's a man alive who could best him in a gunfight. I'm not going after him. Take me to jail," the sheriff said fearfully.

"Sheriff, perhaps you should read my instructions," Timber replied and handed them over the sheriff to read. The sheriff stood there staring at the wall, trembling.

"So, now you see just where you've allowed yourself to get trapped. You can go get Tanner and put him back in the jail cell, or I can shoot you as I've been instructed to do. The choice is yours."

The sheriff dropped into his chair. He looked terrified and began crying. Timber stood there chuckling for a moment and then told him to get up.

"Here's what we're going to do, Sheriff. Put the badge and the jail keys on the desk." The sheriff did as he was instructed, then Timber said, "You have until noon to tell me where Tanner is. Get out there and find him and then beat it back here. I'll drop in now and then to see if you're here. If you don't do as I've just told you, I'll find you and kill you per my instructions. If you do your job on this, I'll let you live. Your choice. Do you understand?" He stood there staring at the sheriff.

The sheriff turned and practically ran out the door. Timber went to the window and watched him run across the street to Keb's saloon. Of course. It made perfect sense. Tanner killed Keb, and then Rogers took control of the saloon with a quitclaim deed thanks to legal eagle Castleman. With that sudden realization, Timber had a feeling there could be a lot more quitclaim deeds filed today and tomorrow and, like it or not, he needed to make sure it didn't happen.

Timber left the jail via the back door and went back the telegraph office. He had shut down the mines because they provided the money used by Winters and Rogers to purchase men and supplies with which they were controlling and destroying the town. Unless he could devise a counterattack, they just might get away with stealing the town from the rightful owners through murder and intimidation. He couldn't let that happen. After giving it some thought, he decided to use a two-pronged attack.

First, he would have the judge seize the mines as part of an ongoing criminal enterprise. It would be new precedent, but he was fairly positive the judge and the governor would give it a try.

Secondly, he would have to delay the filing of any quitclaim deeds. To do that, though, he would need the telegraph operator's help. He explained to the operator that he needed him to somehow make it appear that he was sending the messages but not actually do so, or if he could make it appear as though the line was down, especially if the person sending the messages was affiliated with either Winters or Rogers.

Timber then left the operator to figure out details on his own. He then went to see the doctor. He arrived via the alleyway, moving slowly, checking both in front and behind him as he went. Unfortunately, he never saw the man hiding in the bushes just a few feet away from the front door.

"Morning, Doc," Timber said as he opened the door to the office.

Doc, who had been semi-sleeping in a chair, jumped up and shouted, "What are you doing here? Are you trying to get me killed?" Timber knew right then something was amiss. Timber had been here several times without him reacting this way.

"Whoa, calm down, Doc. I don't think anyone saw me. Besides, who's up this time of day on a Sunday? It's only seven-thirty." Timber went near the window and looked out. "What am I looking for, Doc?" he asked.

"I don't know. It's just a feeling. I've had it for a few days now. This morning, I could have sworn I saw a man among the bushes off to the right, but when I looked back, I couldn't see anything," Doc said.

"We need to check that out. Is there another way out of here?" asked Timber.

"Only the window in my bedroom. Every other way either fronts onto the walkway in or on the street," Doc replied.

"Then I guess the bedroom window it is."

## *CHAPTER FOURTEEN*

The sheriff had run across the street to Tanner's new saloon after leaving Timber at the jailhouse. When he got there, he was surprised to find the bartender was the only person there. He looked up at the sheriff with a blank expression while holding his hand over his six-shooter. Stumbling up to the bar, the sheriff asked to see Tanner.

"You want me to wake Tanner?" the bartender asked nervously.

"I wouldn't ask, except Timber walked into my office not a half-hour ago. He's gunning for Tanner. I need to speak with him," the sheriff begged. The bartender shook his head, then dropped his cleaning rag.

"Wait here," he said and walked off into the back. The sheriff went to the window and stood watching the jail. A minute later, the bartender came back out.

"Tanner said to shut up and sit down. He'll be out in a few minutes," the bartender told him.

"No, that isn't good enough!" the sheriff said loudly. "Timber is going to come walking in here any minute and start shooting. He has a mandate from the territorial governor, dagnabbit!"

Tanner burst through the canvas divider just then, still tightening up his gun belt. He had on his pants, but he wasn't wearing a shirt. The man had muscles on top of muscles. "Didn't I tell you to shut up?" Tanner said to the sheriff. He obviously had a bit of a hangover.

"He's alive and coming for you," the sheriff blurted.

"Speak again before I'm ready to listen, and I'll blow your head clean off your shoulders," Tanner growled as his hand drooped over his gun's handle. The sheriff bit his hand and turned to look out the window. "Get over here and sit down," Tanner ordered. The sheriff walked over and stood next to the table, keeping an eye on the saloon's front window.

"Sit," Tanner snarled.

"Oh, no, thank you. I'd prefer to stand," the sheriff replied.

"I wasn't asking," Tanner spat. The sheriff quickly pulled out a chair and sat down.

"Pour me a coffee and put a double in it," Tanner told the bartender and proceeded to wait in silence for his drink to be brought to him. Within a minute, the man handed Tanner the doctored coffee, and he took a big swig. He savored the flavor. He quickly took a couple more swigs and set the cup down on the table. "Get me another cup with an extra shot of rotgut on the side," Tanner ordered. The bartender jumped right to it. As soon as the bartender set it down on the table,

Tanner downed the shot and began sipping at his second coffee.

"Go see if you can't rustle me up some eggs and bacon," he ordered. The bartender took some money from the till and slipped out the side door. "Now, then, Sheriff, what's got you all flustered this morning?"

"Timber came to my office about an hour ago with a new court order. It was signed by some judge and the governor. They ordered me to recapture you or be declared an outlaw. Timber said he'd let me slide on trying to capture you as long as I found you and told him where you were."

"He told you to find me and you ran straight here. Sheriff, you are absolutely the dumbest man I have ever known. You've led him right to me," Tanner snarled.

"I just wanted to make sure you knew he was here and coming for you," the sheriff replied.

"Gee, as if I wasn't aware he survived my attempt to kill him, and he'd come looking for revenge," Tanner said sarcastically.

"But… now you know when he's coming. Surely that's got to be of some value to you."

"When is he supposed to come charging in?" Tanner asked.

"I don't know. He said something about me going and getting him."

"Okay, then, Sheriff, you go get him, but you'd better be right behind him when he comes through the door, or I'll shoot you myself. And you'd better shoot him in the back the moment he steps all the way into the saloon. If you fail to do as I've told you, I'll plug you so full of holes the undertaker will be able to use you as a wind chime."

"Yes, sir, I'm with you. I'll make sure to shoot him in the back," the sheriff responded as he slowly stepped out of the saloon and headed back across the street. He acted tough for a few seconds, then he peed his pants all the way across the street.

****

Timber slipped out of Doc's bedroom window onto a tight, little space between the doctor's house and next door. He made his way around the far back corner of the house and waited for Doc to do his part. A minute later, Doc stepped out of his door and turned towards the street. When he reached the end of the walkway leading to his office, he turned left. The man in the bushes, no longer able to see Doc, stood up and followed him. Timber quickly stepped out of hiding and, with his gun already drawn, yelled, "That's far enough!"

The man spun around rapidly, drawing his gun as he did, and Timber fired once. The man fell backwards, dead before he hit the ground. Doc came running along with several other people. They gathered around and stood staring down at the man. People began asking if anyone saw anything, but no one admitted they had.

It would go down as another unsolved murder, since everyone knew the sheriff wouldn't make any effort to find the killer. Doc confirmed the man was dead and sent one of the young boys to tell the undertaker to collect the body. Then Doc went through the man's pockets, took off his gun belt and brought everything inside his office. Timber was waiting for him, casually rocking in a padded rocking chair.

"You need to be aware," Timber said, feeling that time was growing short, "that Winters has men stationed under the buildings that are elevated. I'm sure he put them there to ambush Rogers and his men when they come to town. But they'll be able to shoot you down just as easily."

"If anyone saw you, they aren't talking about it," Doc commented as he looked out the window at the body lying on the ground on the other side of the bushes.

"That's good. In a few minutes, though, I expect everyone in town will know I'm alive and collecting bounties. It seems Tanner is in Keb's saloon, which he now owns. I'm going in after him because he's a wanted man for having committed at least six other murders," Timber shared. "With him out of action, Rogers loses a big advantage. But don't let that make you stupid. Any one of the men on either side is potentially lethal. They all have gun skills and have no compunction about killing. These are truly bad men we're about to do battle with. Make sure the whole posse understands that," Timber explained.

"Now, you'll need to organize the locals to get behind the buildings within fifty yards of Winters' compound, especially the ones that are elevated. It's extremely important that those gunmen are taken out first. Put two people on each one to make sure they don't get away. As soon as you have the people in place and the gun battle has started, take them out. Then have your people come up the alleys to the front of the buildings and take cover. You'll know the appropriate time to make your presence known.

"Be extremely careful to keep your conversations as private as possible by not talking too loudly. The men under the buildings will be able to hear you, if you're talking right above them. Be sure to remind the posse that anyone other than posse members and myself should be considered hostile and treated so. In other words, shoot them on sight."

"Timber, we talk about bad men. Men who kill other men. We hold them up as the example of how not to be and yet here we are planning how we're going to kill them without taking them to trial. Aren't we just as bad as they are?" Doc asked out of the blue.

"Where did that come from?" Timber asked.

"The man outside here. I heard only one shot. Shouldn't you have arrested him rather than shoot him?" Doc questioned.

"Doc, I gave him the chance to surrender," Timber said in self-defense. "I called out for him to stop where he was. He chose to spin around and reach for his gun. I had no choice but to fire first and kill him, or it would have been me.

"I've seen many a good man killed by the bad ones because they wanted to allow them a chance for justice. But you need to ask yourself, where is the justice for the victims of these men? They were never given a chance to receive a trial. The bad people take what they want from the good people. They don't earn it or work for it. They steal it. They kill for it. All that keeps our whole world from plunging into darkness is good people realizing that sometimes justice is best served by exterminating the unjust.

"We're serving the greater good today, and we do so with the blessing of the powers that be in the territory. I personally hate killing, but I also happen to hate seeing good people murdered and victimized by the bad people. If I can, I'll take them in for trial, but if they threaten to harm the innocent or refuse to come quietly, I will kill them. In my mind, justice is served either way, and I can sleep just fine knowing I've done my best to make this world a better place."

"You sound like a politician," the doc replied, still looking out the window.

"Whoa, hold on now. Them's fightin' words," Timber snapped playfully before asking, "We good here?"

Doc slowly turned away from the window and looked him directly in the eye. "Yes, we're good."

"Okay. Now, I've got to go and arrest Tanner again without getting killed by him in the process," Timber stated. As he left the doctor's office, Timber grabbed the gun of the man he just shot, tucked it into his waistband and headed back to the jailhouse.

## *CHAPTER FIFTEEN*

The sheriff walked into the jailhouse and froze. Timber wasn't here. He took a seat behind his desk and pulled a half drunk bottle of whiskey from the bottom right hand drawer. Uncorking it, he took a huge swig, letting the burning sensation serve to heighten his senses and calm his nerves. He was sure Timber was setting him up, and Tanner was planning on killing him. He was stuck between a rock and a hard place. He took another big swig and then another, until he'd drunk half of what was left in the bottle.

He needed a third option. Something where he would walk away unscathed by the situation threatening to overwhelm him. As he tucked the bottle back in the drawer, an idea came to him. Why not shoot Tanner in the back? He'd never expect him to have the courage or the guts to try it. Too bad Timber was so suspicious of everyone. He'd never be able to shoot Timber in the back, because Timber would never let him get behind him.

The sheriff checked that his gun was fully loaded and then headed back over to the saloon. He made sure to look up and down the street as he crossed to be sure Timber wasn't sneaking up on him.

****

"Okay, start sending the men into town. Send them in small groups." Mr. Rogers was giving last minute instructions to Mr. Castleman when the first shot shattered the window ten feet behind him. The shot completely missed Mr. Rogers but did manage to pierce a large painting on the wall.

Winters' men were attacking the ranch house and the mine. The attack on them last night had killed more than five dozen men and injured several dozen more. Those who were left were now attempting to kill as many of Rogers' men as possible.

Rogers' men used the fortified walls of the ranch house to their advantage. Once again, they were easily winning the battle until Winters' men began shooting sticks of dynamite at the house and over the walls. They were using bows and arrows to deliver the dynamite with surprising accuracy and devastating results.

"Castleman, keep moving our men to town. The men at the mine can handle these bastards. Winters had to have sent most of his men out here to attack us directly. If we can get men into town, we'll be able to take his compound while it's undermanned," Mr. Rogers directed as they huddled on the floor to avoid being shot by snipers.

"Certainly, sir," Castleman replied and crawled off to set the plan in motion.

Rogers jumped up and ran to the fireplace. He grabbed the 40x-power hunting rifle scope and ran to the nearest window.

Two shots rang out as he moved, but both missed. He began returning fire. He liked to think he was killing men with every shot, but there was no way to tell.

A moment later, Castleman came crawling back into the room. "I have the men assembling behind the house. The men on the roof claim to be enjoying a solid success rate in reducing the number of Winters' men. There are easily a hundred men out there.

"Perhaps you should consider escaping the ranch now while you still can. The dynamite attack is taking a real toll on our forces, and Winters' men are close to breaching the walls in two places. They haven't managed to surround us yet, but they are trying to do so. I fear Winters' men will most likely try to overrun the house very soon."

Castleman was planting seeds of fear in Rogers. He knew they would fester in the petty, arrogant, self-centered man's mind, and then Castleman's plan would be in full swing.

"Perhaps you're right," Rogers shouted over the gunfire and explosions. "Okay, let's head to town and take Winters and his compound, while he's at breakfast."

Mr. Rogers, along with Mr. Castleman and forty men, rode away through a hail of gunfire. As they rode, they cleared a path through Winters' men, leaving twenty men dead in their wake and buying more time for the ranch to hold out and for Winters to fall. They lost five or six men themselves, but they were undeterred. Rogers was convinced that the men left to defend the ranch would succeed in doing so just as they had a month ago. He was equally convinced that he would be successful in taking Winters' compound with the surviving members of his force and the twenty men he had hidden just outside of town. Tanner and his men were a big part of the winning strategy.

****

The sheriff thought he'd be slick and slip quietly into the saloon and nobody would say anything about him coming back without Timber. He was wrong.

"Sheriff, what are you doing here?" Tanner asked the moment the door closed behind him. Tanner was sitting at a table with two other men from Rogers' camp discussing how they could get inside Winters' compound and earn the ten thousand dollar bonus Rogers had promised to whoever brought out Winters for him to kill.

"Timber wasn't over there, and I got real nervous waiting on him," the sheriff replied as he took several steps away from the door.

"I don't care if you have to sit in the corner and suck your thumb, you get your ass over there and wait for him," Tanner growled. "If you come back here without him again, I will shoot you myself. Now get, before I change my mind and shoot you now."

"I'm on your side," the sheriff replied, and Tanner just sat there staring at him. The sheriff accepted his fate and began trudging towards the door. As he reached it, he happened to look up and froze. Timber was walking across the street towards the saloon.

"Oh, God, he's coming this way right now," he practically squealed as he backed up into the saloon.

"Get yourself over here by an outside table. Remember to act like you're with him, and when he draws, you shoot him in the back," Tanner ordered.

****

Timber had arrived back at the jail just in time to see the sheriff cross the street to the saloon, looking all around him as he crossed. Obviously, he was afraid of something. Timber watched as the sheriff hesitated outside the saloon for several seconds before slipping inside, closing the door slowly behind him.

He instantly knew Tanner was in the saloon. He needed to get things done before the rest of Rogers' gang arrived and turned the town into a killing field. Most of the women and children had already left town after the big gun battle last month. Timber reminded himself that if things went according to plan, the townsfolk wouldn't be worrying about another gun battle in their town ever again. If everything went according to plan—that was a big 'if.'

Timber marched into the street in front of the jail and walked straight across to the saloon. He was curious as to why Tanner hadn't already started shooting at him. Then he remembered. Tanner was an extremely fast and accurate gunslinger. He'd want to settle it man to man, gun against gun, to see who was the best. It wouldn't do to be the best and have everyone say, "Yeah, he's good, but he couldn't face Timber, so he shot him through a wall or a door." No, Tanner was inside standing by the bar, waiting to draw down on him.

Timber knew he wasn't the fastest man alive. He was good, faster than most, but he wouldn't call himself amazing. Timber didn't care about any bragging rights. He was here for one reason only—to earn another bounty so he might hopefully earn back his life. He quietly slipped around the corner of the building and snuck around to the side door. He opened the door and quietly entered the saloon.

"Where the hell is he, Sheriff?" Tanner snapped, giving the sheriff a nasty look. When the sheriff didn't respond, Tanner pressed the issue. "Get over there and see!" The sheriff slowly stumbled across the room to a window and peered out.

Meanwhile, Timber had slipped into the storage room. He made his way up to the canvas separating the main saloon from the storage room and listened. He didn't like the fact that, other than Tanner's comments, it was dead silent. He risked a peek through the space between the two canvas flaps. He could see Tanner standing at the bar. The sheriff was against the wall in the far front corner looking out the window. The bartender was standing at the far end of the bar with his left hand on a scattergun. There were two other men sitting with their backs to the storage area. From behind, they appeared to be a matched set of man mountains. They wore the same colored clothes, had on the same style and color hats, and their shoulders appeared to be the same width. They looked a lot like the two he had tussled with a month ago.

"He's not there. He's not there!" the sheriff practically screamed, and the men at the table stood up. Tanner turned towards the storage room just as Timber jumped through the canvas flaps with a six-gun in each hand.

"Hold on there, Sheriff. I'm right here," Timber called out as he cleared the canvas flaps. One of the two men at the table spun around while grabbing for his gun. Timber shot him dead without breaking stride. "That's a shame. Was he valuable to you, Tanner?" Timber asked as the other man at the table stood glaring at him.

"Apparently not as valuable as I had thought," Tanner replied. "Back to arrest me again?" Tanner asked as he turned to the bar, poured himself a shot and downed it. The bartender shifted slightly to get a better grip on the scattergun, so Timber addressed him first.

"Step away from the scattergun. Far away. Stand over by the sheriff," Timber directed him. When the man didn't move, Timber insisted. "If I have to say it again, you're dead." The bartender let go of the scattergun and walked over by the sheriff.

"Now, back to you, Tanner. Why, yes, I am here to arrest you again. It seems there have been some developments regarding your criminal record. Two assaults have been added to it. First is an assault with a deadly weapon with intent to do great bodily harm, including attempted murder on an agent of the court. The second is assault with intent to do great bodily harm resulting in murder. Damn, Tanner, you really know how to assure the court will take great pleasure in hanging you."

"Save all that legal mumbo-jumbo for my lawyer," Tanner snapped as he took another drink.

"Oh, and who might that be?" Timber asked.

"That little knock on the head must have rattled your brain seeing that you've already met him. He had me out in less than a day. I suppose he'll do it again," Tanner gloated.

"Oh, yes, that would be Mr. Castleman, right? I don't think you should count on him to help you out."

"Why is that?" Tanner asked.

"He'll either be in the cell next to yours or the grave next to yours," Timber replied.

"So, are you going to talk me into submission or what?" Tanner inquired. He shifted slightly so he could spin and clear the bar. "You two better get yourselves ready. If I fail to bring him down, you'll need to move extra fast to have a chance to bring him down before he gets you," Tanner told the bartender, the sheriff and the man at the table. "Remember what everyone was saying about how he took on four men at once and beat them all."

"Guns on the floor, gentlemen," Timber called out, but not one of them made any effort to lay their guns down. "Are you really that stupid? I already have my guns out. I don't need to draw, just fire."

The sheriff started to walk towards the front door of the saloon. Timber knew he was running away from the fight, but it was too late for that. He had already chosen his side, and his fate was sealed.

"Hey, Sheriff, you yellow-bellied coward. Where the hell do you think you're going?" Tanner barked.

The sheriff swung around, drew his gun and fired. The shot hit the whiskey bottle on the bar, and it exploded.

At the same time, Tanner spun towards Timber and fired. But Timber had already shot him, firing at the same moment the sheriff had fired. The bullet struck Tanner in the chest as planned. Tanner's bullet hit Timber in the upper right thigh. The man mountain drew his gun and fired at Timber as he fell to the floor. The bartender drew his six-gun from under his apron and also fired at Timber. Both shots missed, high and wide. Timber kept firing as he fell. Both men were fatally shot and fell to the floor, leaving just the sheriff to deal with.

The sheriff stood there frozen, staring straight ahead with his gun in his hand. Despite being the town's sheriff, he had never really been in a gunfight before. Timber's eye traveled over to Tanner. He was kneeling on the floor staring into space. Seeing Tanner was no threat, Timber looked back at the sheriff. He had a look of total surprise on his face.

"Well, Sheriff, it's your move. Put your gun down and things end right here. Keep it pointed at me, and I'll have to assume you're hostile and shoot you," Timber stated loudly in case the sheriff's ears were ringing from the close quarter gunshots. Timber knew his were.

The sheriff continued to stand there wide-eyed as his gun slowly slipped from his hand and fell to the floor. When he tried to talk, Timber could see blood start to dribble out of the corner of his mouth until finally the sheriff fell over face first.

Timber shrugged his shoulders and got up off the floor. He had no remorse for the sheriff. It wasn't as if he had been a good man. He hopped over to the bar and grabbed a bottle from behind the counter, pulled the cork and took a huge swig. It was horrible. It tasted like burnt pine needles. After a second swig, he poured some on his thigh. Although his wound appeared to be just a graze, it still hurt, and the rotgut he poured on it didn't reduce the pain at all. It actually made it worse.

## *CHAPTER SIXTEEN*

Timber reloaded his guns quickly, expecting Rogers to arrive in town any moment now. Of course, he was unaware that Winters' men at the mine had taken it upon themselves to retaliate against Rogers by attacking the ranch house. Timber had hoped Winters' men would attack the Rogers mine also. He wanted to make sure there wouldn't be more than fifty or sixty men fighting it out here in town. As he finished reloading, Timber heard the first gunshots.

Rogers had instructed his men to shoot out every window in every house and business and to kick in every door. If they got any resistance, they were to kill the resisters. Timber wasn't sure if there was anyone left in town who wasn't a combatant and he, like the posse, would be shooting everyone not known to them. As he hobbled towards the front door, he came under fire. He flattened himself on the floor until the riders passed, then he pulled his guns and quickly stepped outside.

It was absolute bedlam. Rogers had men riding up and down the street, shooting at anything and everything that moved. He had other men wandering around on foot, breaking into stores, homes and businesses, looking for people to kill and valuables to steal. A couple of men came out of the gun store with their arms filled with weapons and ammunition. Timber shot them dead. Winters' men joined the mayhem at this point, shooting at the Rogers gang from entrenched positions in front of the wall and upon it. Several men began shooting from the third story of the house and from under the elevated buildings. For a moment, it was devastating to Rogers' men as more than a dozen were killed and close to twenty were wounded. In an effort to catch Rogers' men in a crossfire, Winters sent word to his mine directing the foreman to send his men into town. He wanted to trap Rogers and his men between Winters' compound and the men from the mine. When the messenger arrived at the mine, he found only a handful of men left behind to protect the mine. There were no men to send, so there would be no reinforcements for the men at the compound.

Then twenty men, citizens of Heaven Brook, came armed with shotguns. Per Timber's instructions, they found and then quickly took out the ten men who Winters had stationed under the elevated buildings as soon as the shooting started. Then they moved up the street and began shooting anyone they met. They would strike and then fade back into the buildings, thus keeping the attackers off guard and unsure which way to return fire. The sound of shotguns firing was music to Timber's ears. He knew that nearly every time he heard that sound at least one of the bad men had died. Then he had to account for his own actions. Aside from Tanner and the four other men in the saloon, Timber already had to reload once. He was now back on the street, shooting the raiders as they rode past and the men attempting to pillage the town.

He stood on the edge of the street where he braved the gunfire as he sought out and eliminated random riders spreading chaos riding up and down the streets shooting into the homes and businesses. He also confronted any man he found looting the stores. He had to stop and reload a third time when Mr. Castleman came racing around the corner of a building several storefronts down on Main Street. He must have been hiding in a side alley, waiting for his chance to enter the fray. Castleman was headed straight at him.

Timber finished loading his guns as Castleman charged. He hobbled for cover as Castleman closed in on him. If Castleman had been any kind of shot, Timber would have bought the farm. As it was, Castleman shot his hat off his head as Timber dove behind a water trough. Castleman didn't stop. He just raced by, heading down the street towards Winters' compound.

Timber hobbled down the street clenching a six-gun in each hand and shooting as he went. Halfway down the street, he ducked into a doorway and reloaded yet again. It was the last of his ammunition. When he finally arrived at the area around the compound, he found himself in the middle of an intense firefight, which included men flinging sticks of dynamite back and forth over the compound wall. The explosions were deafening. It didn't take very long until there were only occasional shots being fired. Both sides suffered tremendous losses. It looked as if the entire town had been raked with artillery fire.

Timber was tucked in behind several large crates that somehow had managed to stay stacked in all the turmoil. He had a good view of most of the street including Winters' compound and the burned-out building where Rogers had gone for safety during the gunfight. Timber didn't see Castleman anywhere and wondered if he had somehow managed to escape town in all the excitement.

As Timber sat there, he looked for the citizen posse. He was surprised to see a white flag suddenly pop up on top of the wall in front of Winters' compound.

"Rogers, you still breathing?" Winters shouted from somewhere behind the compound wall.

"It'll take more than you to do me in," Rogers called out in return from somewhere across the street. "You looking to surrender?"

"No, I was going to make you a proposition, though," Winters replied.

"Oh, like what?"

"Like, we settle this like men. We duel it out and the winner takes all," Winters proposed.

"You want to have a showdown with me? Why would you risk it?" Rogers replied.

"I take it you haven't had any reports from the mine just yet. By blowing up my men's bunkhouses and wagons last night, you've inadvertently galvanized the men. I lost over a hundred men. And today, they've informed me that neither you nor I have more than a couple of handfuls of men left. It'll take years for us to recover. That is, unless we have all the resources."

"I didn't send anyone to blow up your bunkhouses. Now that you mention it, I wish I had, but I honestly haven't done so. Besides, it was you who had your men blow up my wagon train last night. The rider was tracked right back here," Rogers shared.

"I didn't send anyone out to your place last night. Hey, what the hell is going on here?" Winters shouted.

"I know what's going on," Castleman shouted from three feet behind where Timber was crouched. Timber had never heard him coming. "Get up," Castleman barked at Timber while poking his back with the barrel of his gun. Timber slowly stood and then hobbled his way off the porch into the middle of the street.

A moment later, both Rogers and Winters emerged from their hiding places along with a half-dozen men, and together they joined Timber and Castleman in the street.

"This gentleman is the saboteur of both your mining operations," Castleman boldly claimed. "Timber caused attacks on both your places last night because he's under the impression the territorial governor wants it done."

"You mean, he's not a bounty hunter?" Winters asked.

"Hell, no. He's a special agent of the court sent to kill wanted men and anyone else he deems as criminal in the territory. The governor wants to clean up the territory before asking for statehood in the United States," Castleman explained.

"How do you know this?" Winters asked.

"I have a friend in the capital who looked into it for me."

"You son of a… " Winters snarled and lifted his gun up to shoot Timber.

"I have a better solution," Castleman quickly interrupted.

"Like what? This snake has pretty much wiped us out. He deserves to die for that," Winters said without lowering his gun.

"Yes, I agree," added Rogers, raising his gun as well and pointing it at Timber.

"Exactly, gentlemen. I believe this would be an excellent way to cement your new partnership," Castleman stated. Both Rogers and Winters stopped, lowered their guns and looked at Castleman.

"What partnership?" Rogers snarled and swung his gun towards Castleman. "Talk," Rogers snapped at him.

"It's really quite simple," Castleman stated as he walked over behind Rogers and Winters, leaving Timber alone across from them. "That man has set the two of you back at least ten years. He's financially ruined you for the foreseeable future. But together, you can rebuild in half the time and become the ultimate power in this territory. Think about it. It makes sense. Kill Timber together, and you'll become twice as powerful as you were before," Castleman explained. Of course, he left out the part about the consequences of killing a Special Agent of the Court. And the little thing about actually being able to kill Timber. He had so far proven to be dang near indestructible.

"You just need to solidify your relationship by killing him, and then we'll sit down and draw up the papers," Castleman suggested, knowing full well they were both thinking they would go along with this cockamamie idea only until they killed Timber and then killed their new partner.

Timber had been silent up until now and wasn't sure what to say at this point. He was ready to draw, but how do you outdraw two men who already have their guns out and are ready to shoot? Plus, there was the minor problem of the twelve other men right behind them who wanted to kill him, as well.

Timber did his best to remain calm as the two power brokers turned towards him. They shared a look that Timber had seen before many times. It was one of murderous intent. Both men began backing away from each other, making it much more difficult for Timber to shoot both of them. They kept moving until they were so far apart, Timber had no chance to shoot more than one of them. The two stood glaring at Timber, their arms outstretched with their guns pointed at him. They remained that way for several seconds. The pressure to fire was nearly overwhelming, but Timber knew that picking one to kill meant the other would kill him. He tried to figure out if he could shoot well enough to draw the second gun and fire it at the same time.

"Okay, now, Rogers. On a count of three," Winters called out.

"Why are you counting? I'll count," Rogers replied.

Timber couldn't help but smirk at the two egomaniacs as they argued over who got to count before they shot him.

"I've already said I will," Winters said.

"Yeah, but I don't trust you!" Rogers bellowed.

"I don't trust you, either!" Winters yelled back.

"Okay, we'll count together," Rogers suggested.

That was the best distraction Timber was going to get, so he joined in. "No, I'll count," he hollered.

Both men turned in unison and shouted, "Hell, no!" and fired. But they didn't fire at Timber. They had turned around and fired at each other, both hitting their mark. What followed was like watching molasses dripping down the side of the jar.

Each man's face took on a wide-eyed expression of shock and surprise, and slowly their guns fell from their hands. They sank to their knees almost in unison before finally falling face down in the dirt, dead.

Timber felt a huge surge of relief wash over his body, and he almost relaxed, until he remembered the twelve men. Timber drew both guns with lightning fast speed and waved them back and forth over the men. Not one raised his gun, but they did raise their hands. Timber wasn't sure what had happened for several seconds until he looked at their faces. They were all focused on something behind him.

Slowly, Timber turned around and found Doc and the citizen's posse standing at the corners of the buildings nearby with their shotguns pointed at the men. No wonder no one dared try to step in. Timber's face broke into a wide grin for a moment, then he remembered there was one more man who needed to be dealt with.

"Castleman? Anybody see where he went?" Timber asked. Nobody said a thing, but Timber had a good idea where he had gone.

## CHAPTER SEVENTEEN

Castleman stood five feet away from the telegraph operator, his gun pointed at the man's head.

"Hurry up and send that message," Castleman demanded.

"I'm trying, but there's something wrong. It just isn't going out," the operator told Castleman.

"Don't give me that nonsense. Now, stop stalling and send it through."

"I didn't think you'd be this big a pain in the ass to work for," Timber said from the storage room behind him. Castleman swung around and fired a shot at Timber then jumped to the other side of the operator, using him as a human shield. When Timber peeked into the room again, Castleman had his gun to the operator's head.

"Don't tell me... you were able to draw faster than those two greedy bastards could pull a trigger?" Castleman asked sarcastically.

"Oh, how I would love to be able to tell you that, but it wouldn't be truthful," Timber said as he stepped into the room, holding his gun in his right hand.

"Not another step," Castleman shouted and bumped the operator's head with his gun. Timber slid his gun in its holster and raised his hands.

"If you shoot him, who'll send the telegram?" Timber asked.

"Shut up," Castleman snarled at Timber.

"I'm just curious. What's the telegram for?"

"The future, Timber, the future."

"What's that mean?"

"Those two fools, Rogers and Winters, were too greedy for their own good. They'd fight over a dollar, while spending a hundred thousand on men and ammunition to fight the battle for them. There are two gold mines out there at opposite ends of the vein. Those mines are worth millions in profits when worked separately and hundreds of millions if combined," Castleman explained.

"So, how is that the future?"

"I was coming to that. It's quite simple, Timber. With the telegram, I become the new sole owner of both Winters #1 and Rogers #1 claims. I'll be combining the two mines into one operation—Castleman #1."

"Isn't it going to be tough to run a mine from a jail cell?" Timber asked.

"Oh, I'm not going to jail, Timber. I'm an attorney. Anything that you think happened between Mr. Rogers and me is covered by attorney/client privilege. You might be able to bring it up in court, but I'll have it thrown out based on attorney/client privilege. I'm not an active participant in this tawdry little drama known as Heaven Brook. I'm an outside advisor who can't be prosecuted under the law for offering advice. Any advice I gave on any subject is privileged information." The telegraph dinged loudly. Castleman smiled and lowered his gun into its holster.

"Sounds like you have this whole thing covered."

"Oh, I have it more than covered. Now, if you don't mind, I have a clean up to get started," Castleman said smugly.

"Whoa, now, hold on there. The charges I have against you have nothing to with your law practice," Timber said. "I'm arresting you for assault with a deadly weapon with intent to do great bodily harm, including murder and kidnapping. I distinctly remember both incidents."

Castleman continued to back away from him towards the front door. "I take it you're going to try a make a case against me based on my celebration in the streets. I must admit, it got a little out of hand, but no one was injured, and I'll be glad to pay for a new hat for you. As far as the kidnapping charge, well, again, I was merely demonstrating the method by which I once saw a bank robbed." Castleman looked at Timber and grinned.

"Mr. Timber," the operator said, "your wire has arrived from the capital, and it's good news."

Castleman looked at the operator as he handed Timber a telegram. "What's that?" he asked.

"So, you shooting at me," Timber ignored Castleman's question, "in the middle of a raging gun battle between two rival gangs, which I suspect you counseled both the gang leaders regarding their actions, was merely a celebration of yours over what? Having not been killed just yet? And what about when you held me at gunpoint and forced me from a place of concealment into a showdown with the two gang leaders—what was that? You providing more counseling?"

Castleman just stood there smiling at Timber as he felt for the door frame behind him, hunting for the knob without taking his eyes off Timber.

"I've got to hand it to you, Castleman. If you get the right judge, you just might get away with it. A little campaign donation, maybe a small piece of the profits for the gold mine, and you're free to go. How am I supposed to counter that?" Timber asked as he stood looking down at the unread telegram.

"You don't, Timber," Castleman offered. "You accept your defeat and move on. Take pride in the fact you were able to bring the majority of those men on your wanted posters to justice." Castleman focused on the telegram in Timber's hand. "Are you going to read that or not?"

"I'm not sure. I already know what it says. I've just been told it was good news. So, I really don't need to read it," Timber said as he continued to toy with the telegram. Another minute passed and just when Castleman started to open the door, Timber said, "Here, you open it. You just might find it interesting." Timber handed the telegram to him. Castleman noticed the operator smirking.

Castleman opened the folded paper and read:

*To: Connors Timber*

*From: The Honorable Judge Milton Westbrook, Chief Justice, Territorial Court*

*Timber,*

*The Territory, as of eleven-fifteen a.m. on the date noted above, has seized the mines known as Winters #1 and Rogers #1 in Heaven Brook. All other claims are officially null and void. Included in this seizure are all properties, livestock, building materials, mining equipment, pre-mined minerals, weapons, horses, personal property except for clothing and one hundred dollars per person, all bank accounts and/or safety deposit boxes, plus any and all other business contracts, properties owned in conjunction or separately by the owners of said mines, Thomas Rogers and/or Gregory Winters, their assigns and/or heirs. All have been deemed fruits of the poisonous tree of criminal corruption.*

*The Honorable Milton Westbrook*

*Chief Justice, Territorial Court*

Castleman's face fell. Everything he had been scheming for was gone—gone before he had a chance to own it. He wasn't a criminal; Rogers and Winters were the criminals. He was an attorney and a very good one. He'd take this seizure to court, and he'd win. There was no precedent for this. There was no new law allowing for it. This damn Judge Westbrook couldn't just make up law as he went. And then there was Timber, the glorified bounty hunter. He'd have to pay for his interference. Castleman crumpled up the telegram and tossed it on the floor. He stood there glaring at Timber, then reached back and opened the door. Slowly, he backed his way through it and out on to the porch. He spun around ready to run, but was met by five men all holding shotguns aimed at him.

He began to tremble. From inside the telegraph office Timber called out, "Castleman, you need to accept your defeat. Be thankful that you almost had it all, and for a while you lived a life most people only dream of. Accept the fact you must now make amends and face the justice you deserve. Now, put your hands up and turn around slowly."

Castleman spun around again, only this time, he grabbed his gun as he went and drew it even before he had managed to come full circle with Timber. Timber had drawn his gun the moment Castleman began to spin. Both men fired a split second apart. Castleman's shot went wide. He had fired before he had squared up. His rage had gotten control of him.

Timber, however, had no issue with rage or with being square to his target. His shot went straight and true, striking Castleman in the chest. The force of the bullet's impact sent Castleman staggering backwards off the porch. He fell three feet to the street where he landed flat on his back, arms and legs splayed to his sides. Doc walked over, checked Castleman's pulse and looked up at Timber, shaking his head from side to side. Castleman was dead.

## *CHAPTER EIGHTEEN*

Timber had to stay in Heaven Brook while the paperwork was filled out and sent off to the appropriate territorial agency for processing and recording. It turned out there were more than a hundred men who were rounded up and arrested and at least a hundred more who rode off, identities unknown. Those they managed to hang onto were charged with a half-dozen crimes including murder, rustling, conspiracy to commit murder, grand theft, arson and racketeering.

The death toll ran to more than two hundred mercenaries and three townsfolk. The townsfolk included Keb, the town's dentist, and the sheriff. All the dead bodies made the undertaker a very happy man and a rich one, too.

Timber made sure the town was awarded possession of the mines, and all the properties that Rogers and Winters had acquired through their various schemes. They were free to do with them as they liked. The town kept them all, and in turn, hired several professional mining engineers, hotel developers, small business managers and lots of labor from back east. Their goal was to get the mine back up and running and jump-start the local economy by starting over two dozen businesses, including a wagon building company, which had a standing order the moment they started work for six hundred wagons to supply the mine. They started a construction firm to build all the new buildings that were needed in town and at the mine, as well.

All told, by the time Timber was ready to move on a few weeks after the second gun battle, the town of Heaven Brook had increased the solid citizen population by more than three hundred people, and they were expecting more than a thousand new faces once the mine was ready to reopen.

"So, Timber, we still have an opening for a sheriff, and the town council still wants to hire you to fill the spot," Doc told Timber as the two of them were having their last drink together before Timber left town.

"I'm flattered, Doc. Really, I am, but I have a commitment I have to follow through with," Timber stated for the umpteenth time.

"How have you been sleeping?" Doc asked.

"Same as always. Two hours on, two hours off."

"That's no way to live," Doc replied.

"It's all I know."

"So, where are you headed next?"

"Somewhere else," Timber said, then finished his drink, got up and walked out of the saloon.

68212043R00083

Made in the USA
Lexington, KY
04 October 2017